I0653123

THE JADED WIDOW

The Jaded Widow
© Nicholas Spill 2020 Miami Beach, Florida

Library of Congress Cataloguing-in-Publication Data
    Spill, Nick
    Crime – Fiction Mystery- Fiction
    Action and Adventure–Fiction
    Thriller–Fiction
    New Zealand–Fiction
    ISBN-13: 978-0-578-75893-0

Book Cover: Angie Alaya
Format and Design: 52 Novels
Author photo: Leon Smith

More information about The Jaded Widow and
the entire Jaded Trilogy can be found at

http://nickspill.com
and
http://nickspill.blogspot.com

THE JADED WIDOW

The Revenge of the Queen of the Auckland Underworld

PART THREE OF THE JADED TRILOGY

NICK SPILL

"Everybody is nice to you when you're dead."

BARBARA "BABS" TURNER

"Toi te kapa, toi te mana, toi te whenua."

WIREMU WILSON, *The Jaded Spy*

"Without language, without mana, without land, the Maori way of life would not exist."

The proverb was the title of a 1972 work by Ralph Hotere, one of the three contemporary Maori artists in Chapter 13.

To Wiremu, wherever you are.
To Joy, beside me with Tristan and Toby.
To Owen, Logan and Ursula who will follow me.

Rangitoto and the Waitemata Harbor from the lower crater on top of Mount Eden, now called Maungawhau.

THE STORY SO FAR...

THE JADED KIWI
AUCKLAND, FEBRUARY 1976

During the great marijuana drought of 1976, Wiremu Wilson, a Maori activist, arranges for a truckload of the coveted crop to be delivered to Auckland. Dr. Mel Johnson meets Wiremu through her boyfriend Henry Lotus. Together with the actress Plum Blossom and violinist Clovis Tibet they help Wiremu escape a police blockade led by Inspector Grimble and form a bond, not suspecting Wiremu's plans for the illegal shipment.

The criminal mastermind Terry Turner and his henchman John Eustace abduct Plum Blossom as a ploy to steal the crop of advanced sinsemilla (very potent marijuana) grown by Plum's cousins, the Look and Wong brothers in Pukekohe.

Hei Hei betrays his cousin Wiremu and seizes the shipment from up north, only to fall into a trap set by Inspector Grimble and the Drug Squad. In a deadly ambush Hei Hei's gang is wiped out in a firefight in a forest near Titirangi, together with four policemen. Dr. Mel uses her martial-arts skills to save Wiremu from being shot by Grimble.

The same afternoon, Turner and Eustace exchange Plum Blossom for a truck full of sinsemilla. On the Southern Motorway they are killed in a giant explosion at a petrol station, set as revenge for stealing the Looks' crop, kidnapping Plum Blossom, and torturing and killing Tony Look. Clovis Tibet rescues Plum Blossom from the inferno.

None of the marijuana reaches Auckland, and the Southern Motorway explosion remains unsolved.

THE JADED SPY
AUCKLAND, AUGUST 1976

Alexander Newton, a curator from the National Art Gallery, has been recruited as a government spy. He photographs a suspected Soviet agent and his contact from the bedroom of a seductive librarian. Alexander escorts a portrait of Captain Cook to the Auckland City Art Gallery. He falls in love with Dr. Mel Johnson whom he meets at the opening of the art exhibition featuring the Captain Cook portrait. When the painting is stolen the suspects include the Soviet agent and Wiremu Wilson, who planned to kidnap the painting to draw attention to Maori land rights.

Mel struggles with her relationship with Henry Lotus, who discovers that his top-secret scientific notebooks have been stolen. Alexander attends Mel's self-defense classes. He tries to win her heart, uncover the truth about the missing notebooks, and save his job as a curator. The Soviet spy plots to kill Alexander and protect his daughter who is a sleeper agent at the local university. Alexander solves the mystery of where the Captain Cook painting is hidden and narrowly escapes a fatal accident by crashing into Inspector Grimble's Honda.

CHAPTER ONE

The only sound was the squeak of the iron hook as it rocked back and forth. A few of the lights flickered, creating a lurid strobe effect over the dimly lit space. The beaten corpse wrapped in chains had fallen onto the dirty floor.

"Shit. He ruined my shoes!" Barbara Turner stomped her stiletto heels. Dressed in a tight leather miniskirt and a pink blouse adorned with a string of pearls, her jet-black hair, usually in a bun, had unraveled. Her lapis-lazuli eyeshadow—hand-ground, specially imported from Australia—stayed immaculate, but her mascara ran down her cheeks in thick dark lines as she glared at her brother.

Michael Donnelly checked his brown brogues, his pressed khaki pants and blue shirt. He appeared out of place in the large garage workshop behind what was now Mrs. Turner's Used Car Sales Emporium on Great South Road in Ellerslie. His ambition and sadism were hidden by the respectable veneer of an accountant, though he was a former rugby player in a puffed-out navy blazer, with a broken nose and cauliflower ears, and his eyes had no life.

He scraped his shoes on a pile of sawdust. The workshop hadn't been cleaned in months. Rags littered the grease-stained floor. Tools hadn't been put back in their place but lay scattered over workbenches or on the ground. There were no vehicles on the three ramps.

Michael stared at the body then turned to his sister at last. "No trace?"

She frowned at her brother, as if he was an idiot. A look he was used to. "Like last time."

Michael smiled. "Got it."

He was the money manager for his sister's enterprises, including the car lot, the laundromats, the massage parlor in Newmarket and the strip club on Karangahape Road. Neither sibling was new to the late Terry Turner's legitimate and illegitimate enterprises they had inherited. Both had remained in the shadows. Michael had created a series of companies and trusts to hide the ownership of their other businesses, except for the used-car lot they now occupied.

Oz the bartender had arrived from Sydney three months ago. He could serve more people faster than anyone else in the club, and he didn't annoy the strippers. Then he took a week off work. A bad case of flu, he claimed when he phoned in sick. The receipts from the two cash registers at the club's long bar showed a doubling of income when Michael tallied all the earnings and compared them to the previous weeks. Michael discovered that the second cash register was used only by Oz, who must have pocketed the cash.

The siblings made a surprise visit to Oz's flat in Grey Lynn. When he opened his front door, Barbara didn't wait for an invitation but marched in. When Oz complained, Michael punched him in the stomach, hard. Fast with his fists and legs, he was overcompensating for his size—and for being John Eustace's replacement in his sister's eyes. He secured Oz's hands behind his back with rope and threw him into the back of his Jaguar XJ6. Barbara took her time getting back into the car. She held a fistful of twenties in her gloved hand.

"How much did you steal?" she shouted as she glanced at the rear-view mirror and drove away. Oz's face was pressed into the backseat as Michael twisted his wrist and arm. "You and I are going to have a little talk."

Michael chuckled and adjusted the rope. He glanced out the window, then at the back of his sister's bun wrapped neatly on top of her head. "I reckon he stole about two hundred dollars a night. He worked for us, what, three months? So about twenty thousand dollars." He gave the bartender's arm an extra twist. "What did you do with the money?"

"I'm sorry," Oz mumbled, then started to sob.

"Shit! Don't let him ruin the leather, Mikey. The car's fucking new."

"Maybe he can float back to Aussie where he came from," Barbara said as she left the workshop. "Knew we should've checked him out further. Probably fled Sydney for doing the same thing."

Michael sauntered to the back where there was a locker room, changed into Wellington boots and overalls, and gathered a few sharp tools and a handful of extra-large plastic bags. Oz had confessed to spending the stolen cash on heroin. The money had gone to a drug dealer Michael supplied.

On Jervois Road he turned right and drove down the hill, his wipers barely keeping his windscreen clear of the rain. He stopped at the bottom of Curran Street, underneath the Auckland Harbor Bridge, and turned off his lights. The rain hammered the roof. He opened the trunk and carefully pulled out a large black plastic bag. He carried it onto the rocks, using a concrete slab for balance. The tide was going out and there was just enough light to see the bag sink. His hair and face were drenched and he could hear the occasional sound of traffic overhead, echoes of tires through the massive network of steel girders. He made another trip with the two smaller bags.

Before he climbed back over the rocks he saw head-lights approaching. He kept still, as any movement might show in the driver's peripheral vision, though he thought he should be invisible in the sheets of rain. The car passed, and he resisted the temptation to peek over the wall and see if it was a police car. He was glad he had shut the trunk and the lights were off. When he sensed the car had gone, he peered over the wall and saw he was alone again. He climbed back onto the pavement shrouded in water.

He scanned the dark water, the empty road, and listened to the noise of the wind and cars above the steel girders. He opened his mouth to taste the rain and savor the sweet air, the smell of the sea. He felt aware of everything around him. The sensations he was experiencing were far more powerful than smoking marijuana with his sister or enjoy-ing a girl from the Flamingo Paradise. He had never felt so powerful, so alive.

Dripping wet, he climbed into his Jaguar and wiped the water off his face. He drove under the bridge, followed the road to the roundabout, turned right by the boathouse, and headed back to the city along Westhaven Drive. He switched his lights on after he saw there were no cars ahead. He prayed his soaked overalls would not stain the soft cream-colored leather seat. Barbara would get upset.

With his wipers at full speed, he thought about his sister and what she would be doing now. Since her husband had been killed a year ago, she hadn't had a boyfriend or lover. When he was fourteen and Barbara sixteen, she had seduced him one night after their parents went out. They had continued their secret affair for several months until she broke it off and found an older, unrelated boyfriend. Michael was furious and jealous at the time. But then, no longer a virgin, he had learned how to please a woman and been given a huge boost in confidence. He wondered if he could ever regain intimacy with his sister, but discounted the idea as a fantasy he had outgrown. He knew this secret would always bind them.

When Michael returned to the workshop he was charged with adrenaline. He dried off with a dirty towel and changed into the business clothes he kept in his Jaguar. He had a visit to make to a girl he was obsessed with at the Flamingo Paradise which closed at two in the morning. Her name was Tiffany.

CHAPTER TWO

Alexander parked the small, white government van on Kenya Street, in the suburb of Ngaio, facing back into town. He was a mile away from the house. A black watch cap kept his long hair in place. He was a jogger and felt invisible in a dark tracksuit despite his six-foot three-inch frame and wide shoulders. He took long strides and turned right onto Crofton Road. There were no vehicles and no pedestrians out this late. He struggled on the hill and stopped to gain his breath. He turned the bend and came to a long driveway almost hidden with trees and shrubs. Then he saw the trade unionist's house: there were no lights on. He walked toward the front door, slowing his heartbeat.

At the steps, he stopped to listen. His breathing had returned to normal. The house was dark, silent. He put on leather gloves. As instructed, he found the front-door key under the second flowerpot to the left. He slipped the key into the lock, carefully opened the door and eased his way inside, leaving the door slightly ajar and the key in the outside lock for a quick exit. He stepped inside then stopped when a small white Scottish terrier approached him, growling.

Alexander eased his body to the carpet and extended his right hand. The dog stopped, looked at the stranger and slowly walked to his fingers. Was the dog going to bite him or bark? Either way Alexander would run, and the dog would probably chase him down the street. He hadn't been briefed about the dog, and his three previous trips to surveil the neighborhood had failed to identify any pets.

Alexander stroked the dog behind its ears. The dog rolled over and he rubbed its stomach. He kept one eye on the corridor that led to the bedrooms. If his new best friend behaved, he would have time to complete his mission.

The first union job had been easier. His boss, Richard Catelin, the Permanent Under-Secretary for the Department of Internal Affairs, had given him a file with a photo of Doug McLeish, the charismatic secretary of the New Zealand Trades Council, and a photo of his famous 1956 Chevrolet Bel Air. McLeish always drove his shiny red car to government meetings. In the file was a photograph from the *Dominion* newspaper of McLeish by his vintage car, beaming his wide worker's smile. McLeish was to appear at a critical meeting the next day with the Prime Minister: if the talks failed, the Seamen's Union, the Drivers' Union and the Harbor Board Workers had planned a mass march from the inter-island terminal to Parliament.

Alexander had crept to the car parked in McLeish's driveway. At 2 A.M. all the houses on the street were dark. Wearing leather gloves, he knelt by the left rear bumper and turned the metal knob at the top of the taillight. He had been briefed on how to open the hidden fuel cap. It wouldn't budge. He had to use both hands to force it to turn before he could pull back the light fitting and find the fuel cap. The hinge made a loud squeak he thought would wake the neighborhood. He froze, his eyes scanning the houses to see if any curtains moved. He held his breath.

When he realized no one had heard him, he went back to examining the open taillight. Relieved there was no lock on the fuel cap, he twisted it off and placed it in his pocket. He took a plastic funnel from his jacket with his other hand and poured water from a large plastic bottle he produced from his other pocket. Once emptied, he replaced the bottle with another and poured the contents into the tank. A car cruised past, and Alexander kept very still. The car did not stop and once the street sounded deserted again he took his last water bottle out of his jacket and poured it into the tank. He put the bottles and funnel back inside his jacket, secured the cap and closed the taillight without the hinge making a sound. He backed out of the driveway on his knees before he got to the street. No curtains moved, no lights went on, no dogs barked. He stood, looked around and slowly walked to his van parked around the corner. He threw the funnel and water bottles into a garbage bin in the city and drove to his apartment in Thorndon.

Next morning McLeish's prized car stalled at the end of his street. The photographer, hoping to get a shot of McLeish driving from his house, instead caught him kicking his tires and pulling at his hair. The photo was on the *Dominion*'s front page next day, mirroring the unions' frustration with the National government's position against new wage increases. The labor talks were a failure and the unions marched on Parliament.

Now the Scottish terrier rolled over and padded off to its water bowl in the kitchen, allowing Alexander to stand next to the large aquarium between the living room and the open kitchen. He took a bottle out of his jacket, undid the cap, and made a small gap at the top of the metal cover to the aquarium so he could pour its contents into it.

A gust of wind blew the front door open then it slammed shut. The dog jumped and barked. Alexander heard noises from a bedroom—someone was getting out of bed. He eased the metal top back into position and, gripping the bottle, made himself as small as possible behind the aquarium.

Heavy footsteps came down the corridor in slippers. If the man turned on the lights and searched the house, Alexander planned to leap up, push him over, grab the door and run as fast as he could. He heard the dog greet its owner and footsteps to the front door. Then a grunt. A light went on in the hallway. If the heavy man found the outdoor key in the front door, Alexander was screwed.

Alexander shut his right eye to preserve his night vision and saw with his left he was still in darkness. The light from the doorway was switched on and the front door was opened then shut again. The light must have temporarily blinded the man, who walked back to the kitchen. Alexander heard the refrigerator door open and the man drinking something from a bottle. From where he crouched he could not see anything, but heard the dog's paws on the kitchen linoleum.

Alexander calculated he had not poured enough liquid into the aquarium to cause any immediate damage, in case the man came to check his fish. Then he sensed the man on the other side of the tank. He could hear the man's breathing as he stood there for some time, only a few feet away. Then the man burped, turned off the hallway light from another switch and shuffled to his bedroom. A mattress creaked, there were some muffled words then nothing.

Alexander let out his breath slowly, opened his right eye and tried to calm his heartbeat. He felt the dog come back to sniff his trousers. He stayed there and used one hand to steady himself and the other to stroke the terrier, who seemed delighted with the attention and wagged its tail.

When the dog lost interest in having its ears rubbed and returned to the kitchen, Alexander rose and surveyed the living room and kitchen. He half expected to see the man with an axe handle waiting on the other side of the tank but there was no one. A couple of fish floated upside down on the surface. He gently lifted the lid again and squeezed the rest of the contents of the bottle into the water. He re-arranged the lid, stepped sideways and took a peek at the hallway. He could see no lights and the dog was still in the kitchen busy licking itself.

He saw the liquid spread through the tank. He did not want to witness what would happen next.

The dog returned to stare at him. He knelt to pat it again, then retreated to the entrance. He put his finger to his lips as if to tell the dog to be quiet. The terrier wagged its tail. For a moment Alexander thought it would bark as he approached the front door. He opened it with both hands and closed the door slowly, being careful to twist the key and lock the door. He returned the key to the correct flowerpot and made sure the key pointed to the door, the way he had found it.

A flash of lightning lit up the driveway. Thunder shook the house. He lifted his head and caught the first drops, then it poured as he walked then ran to the road. He patted the empty bottle inside his drenched jacket. The wind had gotten stronger as it swept his face and he could taste the purity of the water as he jogged to his van.

Alexander recalled the big red book Under-Secretary Richard Catelin had lent him. *KGB: the Secret Work of Soviet Secret Agents* by John Barron. Was he part of the New Zealand version of Department V? Not really, he figured—he had not assassinated anyone, just stalled a classic American car and killed a few fish.

.   .   .

"I didn't wake you, did I?"

"Alexander? Alexander! It's three o'clock in the morning. Why would you think I'd be awake? I was in a deep sleep."

"I just wanted to hear your voice. Sorry, I can call back tomorrow." Alexander surveyed the deserted street from the red phone box on Willis Street, a pile of coins in his hand. The light was broken and he was in darkness.

"Are you nearby?"

Alexander sensed a longing in her voice. He closed his eyes and imagined her naked in bed, her long curly hair falling over her wide creamy shoulders.

"I wish. I'm in Wellington. It's supposed to be summer but it's cold, wet and windy. I miss you."

"Well, you should try calling at a reasonable hour."

"Don't hang up. I'm planning on flying in next weekend. Can I stay at your place?"

"Of course. In fact, you might be able to help me with something I'm working on. I need your help."

"Help?" Alexander's mind started to race.

"We'll talk when I pick you up. Call me back when you know your arrival time. During daylight hours!"

She hung up and Alexander listened to the buzzing sound. He placed the receiver back in its cradle, scooped his coins and walked to the van. He no longer felt cold and miserable. What was Mel referring to? He was excited at the thought of seeing her again but apprehensive as to his reception.

It felt like months, not weeks. He had been erratic in his communications. He had sent her chocolates, red roses, love letters, even a poem and a photo he had taken for her in Wellington, but he was uncertain how she felt and feared he was overreaching. Alexander had no idea how to behave with her because he had never felt these emotions before. All he knew was that the long-distance relationship was doomed.

He had to do something to sustain his friendship, his intimacy, his need for Mel. He was always thinking of her, in bed, on the carpet, that night in his van at the top of Mount Eden. He wished he had taken photos of her in the moonlight as she swept her long hair behind her. The way she looked without makeup, completely natural but gorgeous. He had never seen her with eye make-up, and maybe only once did she wear lipstick; her lips always appeared red and full. Lips he could not stop kissing. The way she used her hands to tie her hair back, fixing him with her amber eyes.

He shuddered as he replayed these images to reassure himself she was real and hoped she would run into his arms when she saw him again. He knew the only way their relationship would work would be for him to move to Auckland and find a job at a gallery.

CHAPTER THREE

Inspector Bernie Grimble admired the view of Mount Albert and the suburbs from the edge of the parking lot for the Department of Scientific and Industrial Research complex. Rows of wooden single-story homes in manicured quarter-acre sections stretched out to the blurred horizon, between parks and roads, dotted with mature Norfolk pine trees. There were only two small clouds in a brilliant azure sky. Despite the haze they could see Mount Eden and in the distance the vague shape of Rangitoto, the symmetrical volcanic cone that seemed to float in the Waitemata Harbor.

"Thank you for meeting us." Grimble moved away from his 1972 dark blue Ford Falcon, unfolded his bare arms and rose to his full height to shake the hand of a thin, bespectacled man with white tufts of hair on his head that made him look like a well-trimmed poodle.

Grimble introduced Detective Sergeant Cadd, who with longer blond hair, sideburns and deep blue eyes would have been handsome, but his face had seen too many rugby scrums. Like Grimble, he was dressed for the hot February weather in white shirt, thin tie and gray slacks.

"It's easier out here, not so many eyes and ears," the man in the oversized lab coat muttered. "You have my report. What else do you want?" He adjusted his wire framed glasses and looked back at the building as tiny strands of hair blew across his face from the breeze on the hill.

"Well, that's it, isn't it?" Grimble attempted a smile. "Not everything finds its way into these government reports. I know—I have to write them. But we are interested in what you *didn't* put in. What you thought."

The scientist pulled a long face. When he stuck his hands in the lab coat, his shoulders disappeared.

"Well. There were certain things I left out, couldn't prove. I didn't want to ruffle any feathers. We were told to wrap it up quickly and keep it brief."

"What did you leave out?" Grimble asked in the silence as he snuck a glance at Cadd.

"For a start, there were no taggants. We didn't find any microscopic polymer or metallic particles to identify the explosive, so it wasn't C-4. I think it was Semtex, from the Czech Republic. Commies. They don't use identifiers. It's used in terrorist attacks. So it probably came from Vietnam. Our boys, the Grey Ghosts, could have brought it back. Whether official or not, I have no idea, so I didn't include it.

"Which brings me to my next point. We took samples of mud from around the explosion on the Southern Motorway. The fire trucks used so much chemical foam and water any possible evidence was washed away as were the detonators. There was probably several detonators for such an explosion—or rather explosions. I think there were at least two, but it's difficult to prove.

"We sifted through buckets of mud, then finally we found these little organic balls. Well, they're not balls, they're seeds. Dark, hard but not burnt." He looked back at the building, the windows, the front entrance. A young man walked to his car on the other side of the car park.

"Well? You said seeds?"

"Yes." The scientist watched the car pull away then turned back to the detectives.

"You're going to have to tell us what they are," Grimble said.

"I had no idea what they were, so I took some samples to a colleague at the university."

Grimble's eyebrows, already close at the best of times, came together.

"Turned out he knew right away what they were." The scientist surveyed the two policemen. "But he didn't say how he knew."

"Well, what were they?" Grimble had to ask.

"He had an electron microscope, so after he brushed off the soot or exterior damage, he could tell they were sativa seeds. Now, what was odd was we never recovered many seeds. Just a handful and we sampled a lot of soil, burnt asphalt, mud—anything we could dig up in a grid around the entire site of the explosion. If the truck had been full of marijuana, dried and cured, you would expect a lot more seeds."

"What are you getting at?"

"The truck most likely contained sinsemilla, specially grown female plants with no seeds. They are cultivated very carefully and haven't been pollinated, and therefore haven't any seeds, but are just chock-full of THC. It's an extremely potent blend. So, being the scientist I am, I came back here and I conducted my own experiment. Here, follow me."

"Would the seeds grow if they had been burnt?" Grimble asked.

"Interesting you should ask, as the guy at the university thought the seeds were too damaged to use. But no, they wouldn't and these . . . Well, see for yourself."

The scientist led them around the back of the two-story brick building on a narrow, unmarked path and through a gate he unlocked. They followed him on a path behind a building with no windows and came to a small garden enclosed in high wire fencing. He unlocked another gate and walked through rows of giant tomato plants. He stopped at a cluster of two-meter tall dark-green plants with serrated leaves and balls of multicolored buds.

He waved his hands at the crop. "There. The proof is in the growing."

Grimble and Cadd widened their eyes at the huge plants. "Holy shit!" Cadd breathed out. "The smell!"

"For scientific purposes only, of course." The scientist grinned as he walked down a row of tall plants. "We have a license."

To Grimble the scientist did not look like his idea of a typical marijuana user.

"See? I've trimmed them, of course. They're all females. Trying to generate as much juice as possible to attract males. Those buds! Have you ever seen anything like this?"

The scientist shuffled his feet as he stopped between the two policemen. "The expert you really need to talk to is the arson investigator for the Australia New Zealand Mutual Providence Society, or ANZMUPS as I call it. His name is Lance Beefeater."

"Beefeater? With a name like that he has to be good."

"He comes across as a country bumpkin, a rich farmer's son. Talks in clichés, too friendly and back-slapping, you know the type of bloke?"

Grimble nodded.

16

"It's an act. He's the best in the business. Lives in Hamilton so he can be near his dad, who's an alcoholic, but he travels to Auckland for any questionable fire and he loves explosions."

They stood in the cathedral-like enclave. The plants seemed to be growing as they talked, Grimble thought.

The scientist pulled out a business card from the breast pocket of his lab coat. "Call him, but he's better in person."

"And we never saw this." Grimble turned to leave, bumping into Cadd who stood inhaling the pungent aroma.

The scientist was about to return to his office when Grimble called him back. "By the way, what did you mean when you said the man you saw at the university knew straight away what they were?"

The scientist turned around. "He's an expert."

"What's his name? What department?"

Cadd made a note of the details.

"We do get the oddest requests," the scientist continued. "Had some spook from Wellington here the other day asking about putting sugar in a car's petrol tank."

"What did you tell him?" Grimble asked.

"Sugar doesn't dissolve in gasoline, so it's a myth. Doesn't work. If you want to sabotage a car, use water. A gallon of water will stall a car in a few minutes but not do permanent damage if you drain the tank."

"Yes, you *do* get the oddest inquiries."

"Can I go now?"

"Thank you, you've been most helpful." Grimble turned his lips up, almost a quick smile.

CHAPTER FOUR

"Do you think this is safe?"

"Ricky, we're in an old wooden hut, away from the last greenhouse and far from our dead-end road. No one knows what's here."

"What about her?" asked Chuck.

Bruce Look glanced at his younger brother. "Why are you worried about her? She has no idea what we're doing. For all we know, she never knew what her husband did before you blew him up."

"And let's not forget your brother Tony," Ricky shot back. As a Wong, he towered over his nephews with his barrel chest and massive arms.

"Oh, come on," said Chuck. "We've both lost brothers. We have to think of the future. We have a lot to gain here—let's not squabble."

The Looks and the surviving Wong were third-generation New Zealanders with classic Chinese features. Bruce Look was older than his brother by three years, was shorter and moved and spoke deliberately. Chuck spoke faster and was agile in his movements even though his eyes were bloodshot.

The three men stood by the doorway of the wooden hut whose high, rusted, corrugated-iron roof had vents around the top for air flow. It was cool and dry, in the shade of a large pine tree, and the space appeared much bigger inside. They could see their entire cured harvest encased in sealed glass jars, usually used for jams and preserves, stacked in rows. Each half-gallon jar held about fifty grams of buds with space to spare at the top. The gallon jars were stuffed with leaves, sticks and other debris and held roughly one hundred grams, but Chuck had discovered that weights varied depending on how much moisture was in the buds and how dense they were.

On another long series of shelves at a lower level were double-wrapped plastic bags. The aroma leaked from these, and Chuck estimated they would dry out, and the buds would break up and lose their potency. The same could be said for the buds in the glass jars. Chuck did not want to open all the lids and let them air out for a few minutes before resealing them. He wanted to sell them. The product, as they called it, was jammed with multi-colored buds. Purples, deep reds and greens as dark as night shone out of the packaging.

"I'm thinking we should call the harvest Purple Haze. It's pure sativa. All buds, well, in the jars here. Remember our selling points: genetically designed for a slow, long, smooth high. A cool smoke. See the density of these buds? They're almost lavender in color. No one has ever seen anything like it before. We sell a minimum of four jars per customer. And use gloves when handling these, always. Remember? Prints on glass will last."

"What do you mean genetically designed?" Ricky asked.

"Didn't you invent the term?" Chuck shot back.

"Yeah, but it's bullshit. There's nothing genetically altered here."

"It's good marketing. Buyers love to hear this. If they think they're going to get a special high, well, they will. What do they know? They're stoners."

"What if she knows?" Bruce repeated. "Our sergeant in Pukekohe says she knows everything. She sends people to spy on us."

"Time to get guard dogs?" Ricky asked.

"They'd only draw attention to us back here. You know how people talk. It would seem we had something to hide. Something valuable. Whoever heard of guard dogs for lettuces?" Bruce shrugged. "Our neighbors are paranoid enough about us already."

"Yeah. Probably right. But we got to sell our crop now. Get rid of it. You realize we won't get full market price? Below wholesale, if we're lucky."

"But we've invested so much, and the seeds we had to buy."

Chuck made a face. "Hey, *I* got those seeds. Our cousin the scientist at uni."

"What about him?" Ricky asked.

"Well, he originally wanted a cut from the total harvest as well as cash upfront this time. But I talked him out of the percentage. Difficult to calculate." Chuck opened out his hands. "Besides, we paid in cash last time so I did the same here."

Ricky spoke again. "Do you think he could give us up?"

"No way. He's got too much to lose, with his salary, his pension. Besides, he's family." Chuck looked at Ricky. "Why are you so jumpy?"

"I just want to offload everything now. Aren't you nervous about having so much product here?"

"We're going to sell it in good time," Bruce said. "We're not giving it away."

"Then who are our buyers?"

Bruce frowned. "We have someone we talked about, right? Ricky?"

"It's ironic, isn't it? Last year we were tricked into thinking the Wilsons were about to steal our harvest and now we're going to use them to distribute. Do you still think it's a good idea?"

Bruce stared at Ricky. "Do you trust Moana?"

"Yes. Of course. She's my girl. She would never screw me or my family."

"Then why the face?" Bruce asked. "It's dark in here. Let's lock up and go outside. I'm high just from breathing."

Chuck locked the door to the shed and looked around the paddock and the slight rise in the near distance. An unpaved track led to their family home, hidden behind the small hill. The brothers could drive from the house down to the greenhouses, in between rows of lettuces and other vegetables, and park under the large pine tree that provided shade in the afternoon for the storage hut. The air was fresher outside and warmer.

Ricky stepped out of the shade of the big pine tree and looked around at the four greenhouses, then back at the two Looks. He stretched out his arms and yawned.

"It's just, Wiremu and his brother Rawiri. Good to have as friends, allies, but dangerous as business partners. If anything went wrong we would pay, not them." Ricky folded his arms and his biceps looked even bigger.

"What could go wrong?" Chuck asked. He scanned the very limited horizon. Even someone watching the greenhouses with binoculars from the road would not be able to see them where they stood.

"You name it." Ricky shrugged. "For a start, our greedy bastard Sergeant Bradshaw. We've paid him, what?"

"It's five thousand dollars so far. And now he wants another five." Bruce spotted an ant in the grass carrying, for its size, a large piece of dirt. Then he saw another ant with a larger piece of dirt.

"Again?" Chuck whistled. "He didn't do much last year, did he?"

"He's our safety net," Bruce said. "He can't turn us in, can he, or he'll go down with us. I took photos of all the cash we gave him. Hundred-dollar bills. I can prove we gave him the money. I have a tape recording as well. It would not be good for him."

"You did?" Ricky asked. "Where are they?"

"In our safety deposit box. I have them in the house too."

"There are some cousins in Wellington who'll take anything we can supply them with," Ricky said, "but they want a heavy discount."

"Yeah, family discount." Bruce raised his hands. "But seriously, better to keep it in the family and not give the Maoris so much."

"Aren't they growing their own up north?" Chuck added.

"Yeah. Moana explained it to me. But they want to sell different types. It's all about consumer choice. And they have control over most of the pot in Auckland. 'Most' is maybe a little optimistic. But if we don't get into business with them, there are some really hardcore gangs out there. The Mongrel Mob, Hell's Angels, Black Power. Do you want to do business with them?"

"Are you prejudiced cos they're Maori, Ricky? I thought you were good with your girlfriend. Is there something you're leaving out?"

"No, just trying to be careful. Last year there were five of us. Now we're just three. It sobers you up a little. What we're getting into."

"A little, you said? Too late now for any regrets, isn't it?" Bruce watched the ant with the biggest payload of dirt climb through the grass.

CHAPTER FIVE

Alexander's eyes wandered over the poster of Gustav Klimt's *Danaë*, half obscured by a red lampshade covered in lace. He thought Deborah was more voluptuous and sensual than the woman in the poster. And she was spread out next to him. He had never experienced such moments of ecstasy before, fueled by alcohol. Caressing her body, her thighs, her long red curls over his face and shoulders, with the red and gold fabrics around the wooden-posted bed, the soft lighting and Erik Satie usually playing in the background and the sandalwood incense, always the incense, and for a moment he wondered how could he live without her. Yet he was in a cold damp flat at the bottom of the world, across the road from the house of a dead Soviet spy, and he still didn't know her last name.

Alexander was addicted to Deborah the librarian, her easy seductiveness, the way she gave herself to him within minutes of seeing him. How could he live without her erotic force? He wondered what would happen when he flew to Auckland. How would he handle Mel? Tell her everything—or nothing?

He turned to the matter in hand, dealing with Deborah and all her temptations. His instincts told him something was amiss. "Let's play a game. It starts with saying, 'What's it all about?'"

"What's what about?" Deborah snuggled closer to Alexander and almost knocked over his Southern Comfort on his bare chest. "For example?"

Alexander grabbed the glass. "I say, 'What's it all about?' And you say . . ." He waited for a response, but Deborah frowned at him. Her thick red curls partially obscured her breasts and pale skin. She was so different from the stern librarian who had ascended the stairs to her flat an hour before.

"Redheads and Southern Comfort." He sighed.

"Oh. I get it. Say it again." Deborah shook her hair, causing Alexander to gently remove strands from his nose.

"What's it all about?" He kept a neutral expression.

"A handsome spy with a camera and a dead doctor."

"What?" Alexander straightened, caught his glass, hesitated as he scanned her face, then emptied his drink in one gulp. Staring into her eyes he ignored her body, her flaming hair. He was concerned.

"Well, that's you and your camera and my neighbor, Doctor Summer. He died while you were in Auckland."

"What?" Alexander repeated, trying to keep his voice from rising an octave. He exhaled. "You knew all along?"

"I know my neighbors. I read newspapers, and as you said, I'm a certified keeper of the sacred Dewey system. I love the title."

"I should give you another title." He went to kiss her, but she stood.

"I'm going to get more Comfort. Want some?"

"Same again, please."

He was too busy thinking, when she returned, to marvel at her round white bottom as she switched on her turntable. In their haste to get into bed, she had forgotten the music. He watched as she placed the needle on the record. She adjusted the volume to counter the sound of the rain and wind now banging on the windows.

She turned to see him watching her. "I knew all along. I wasn't going to spoil it for you. It was fun."

"Yes." He paused for a moment and took a sip of his drink. "Was?"

"Is, silly." She slid her body on top of him and her hair cascaded over his face. The light from the red lace over the night lamp made her hair seem on fire. He breathed in her smell, slightly acidic but of flowers mixed with sweat and lust, and closed his eyes. He held her tight, his arms around her back.

"Oh god." He tried to breath as he opened his eyes again. "What's this album?"

"It's Split Enz. *Mental Notes*."

"And the track?"

"Hmm, think it's called 'Stranger than Fiction.'"

"Well, that's appropriate, isn't it."

"Remember, I'm a librarian. I know everything."

"Do you? I'm flying to Auckland, speaking on maraes. Part of the travelling show I'm organizing."

"You're talking on a marae?" Deborah eased off him and placed her hand on his chest.

"Yes. Don't sound so shocked."

"Can you speak Maori?"

"Well, I can say 'kia ora'. And 'where's the kai?' Why are you laughing?"

"Do you know anything about Maori protocol, kawa, when visiting a marae?" Deborah sat up. "You need to know all this, and learn some Maori, otherwise you're going to look stupid."

"I can do stupid with my hands tied behind my back."

"Seriously. You won't get what you want if you don't follow the rules."

"Oh. Can you teach me?"

"I can do better. I can coach you what to say and when. I've spent a lot of time on maraes, I'm about one eighth Maori and, most important of all, I have a book. It's important if you want to make a good impression."

Alexander became sober immediately at the thought of talking in Maori on a marae.

He absorbed everything Deborah told him and repeated the correct pronunciation, recalled the sequence of events and phrases he had to memorize, and recited his opening speech in Maori, despite all the alcohol he had consumed. He took notes and wrote out his speech on cards she provided him.

Pleased with his progress, he sipped his drink and watched her bend over to change the record. He could not keep his eyes off her. Having a naked tutor somehow helped him learn.

"I can't believe you knew all along. You fooled me."

She pulled the curls from her face. "You told me you were doing a random photography performance or some such thing, and I didn't want to question you. I was preoccupied." She stood at the edge of the bed and gazed at him. She tied her hair back with a ribbon and held his eyes.

"So was I. I still am." To Alexander she was luminescent standing there, uninhibited. She sighed and climbed back into bed.

He glanced at the windows. Rain hammered the glass. He had scanned the street before he parked his van and had seen no suspicious vehicles.

"And you knew about me? How?"

"It was no coincidence you were opposite his house." Deborah kept a straight face.

Alexander waited for an explanation. He watched as she sipped the drink she had rested between her breasts.

"Who told you about me, then?"

"Remember, I'm a librarian. We know everything." She undid her ribbon and her hair fell back over her face and a small smile emerged. "I worked it out myself."

"You did?"

"Yes." Deborah pushed her hair back again and pulled the sheet to cover her chest. She kept her eyes on Alexander.

"I don't believe you." He stared at her and her hands gripped the sheet.

"It's just you and me." She purred as she batted her eyelashes.

Alexander was quiet for some time as he kept his gaze on her. "Have you told anyone?"

"It's our little secret."

Alexander felt a wave of dread course through his body. He was unsure about what she had told him, and the exact words she had used. An image came to him of the two used scotch glasses in Catelin's office but then he recalled the lingering smell of Old Spice. He wondered what the connection was.

He turned again to her innocent face framed with long red curls. "What happened to the doctor? How did he die?"

"All I heard was he had a heart attack. Nothing else. No rumors or anything. Why? Do you know something?" It was Deborah's turn to stare at him.

He looked into her fierce green eyes and blinked.

CHAPTER SIX

"You were right about running all the accident reports after the explosion." Detective Sergeant Cadd dropped a pile of folders on Inspector Grimble's desk then carefully placed a typed summary on top.

"Yes. Well?" Grimble took the summary in his right hand and knotted his eyebrows at his sergeant.

"There are some interesting connections."

"Let's stop right there." Grimble dropped the summary and raised his hand. "Both cases are officially closed. I don't think we're going to dig up anything to help our current investigation. I've just talked to Thompson."

"The former commissioner?"

"Let's be honest, Cadd. In both the Titirangi shootout and the Southern Motorway explosion, all the criminals are dead. Cases closed. We have to concentrate on Mrs. Barbara Turner, the widow. She's our link to this network, if there is such a thing. Because we think she's running everything now. How do we discover what she's doing?"

"There's Plum Blossom. She worked at the Flamingo Paradise and was rumored to be Terry Turner's mistress. She was somehow linked to the explosion on the Southern Motorway."

"We have to see her. Got her address? And also what's-his-name, the tall violinist."

"Clovis Tibet."

"Yes, how could I forget a name like that."

"Wouldn't Vice know about the Flamingo Paradise, sir?"

"Good question, but just as we're not involving the Drug Squad for now, let's leave Vice out of it. Who knows if she has any influence with them? Do you have anyone you trust there?"

Cadd appeared to think for a moment. "There's one more thing, sir."

"What?"

"You asked the scientist with the pot forest about the other scientist at uni with the electron microscope. Aren't we going to follow up with him?"

"I thought about it. But what if Mr. Wong with the electron microscope had supplied the seeds to the Looks? Wouldn't he call them and alert the Looks that we're investigating them? I think we can assume he was their supplier. It's something we haven't come across before. This level of sophistication in growing plants. Sinsemilla."

Cadd shrugged. "We could ask the Drug Squad but you don't want to?"

"Right. The Looks have the horticultural know-how. They're not ordinary hippies or Maoris growing cannabis in the wild. Means we have to check out the Looks and see what they're doing now. It's February, late summer. Maybe they've harvested already."

"Then we might be too late?"

"Come on, Cadd. An investigation is like a shark. We have to keep moving forwards."

CHAPTER SEVEN

Sergeant Cadd had located Plum Blossom and Clovis Tibet on Lincoln Street, one short block from Ponsonby Road. He and Grimble surveyed the street dressed in their unofficial detective uniform: short-sleeved white shirt, narrow dark tie and gray slacks. There was a white picket fence and a few bushes in the front garden; everything looked in need of paint and repairs.

Grimble knocked on the front door. Plum Blossom peeked through the side window then opened the door. Grimble attempted a friendly smile, introduced himself and his sergeant then stepped inside, uninvited. Plum Blossom had no option but to lead them into the living room. The two policemen looked around the bare room and sank into a red velvet sofa, their hands on their knees. The wallpaper, curling at the edges, had been painted white. The floor was a dull polished wood. A tall music stand was near the window by a pile of sheet music.

They stared at Plum who gazed at them, a fixed smile on her innocent-looking face. Her thick black hair almost covered her eyes in an overgrown pageboy haircut. With no make-up and wearing what looked like an oversized T-shirt, Grimble thought she could pass for a schoolgirl. He tried shallow breaths—there was a smell he recognized coming from the sofa. Cat piss.

"Have you been to Pukekohe recently?" he asked. "How's your grandfather?"

"Fine, thank you. Still gardening and talking about the rain."

"How's Clovis? Is he here?"

Cadd glanced at Grimble, trying to hide his surprise at the inspector's friendly tone.

"No, he's rehearsing." She smiled. "He's in the Auckland Symphony Orchestra."

"He plays the violin, correct?"

"Yes."

Grimble looked over at the sheet music. "Wonderful. My daughter plays as well, but I never get to see her perform. Only practice at home."

Plum Blossom kept her head down, and after a long moment, Grimble said, "I remember you're an actress, right? Have you been in any plays lately?" He attempted a smile. "Anything planned?"

Plum shook her head no.

Grimble changed his tone. "Plum, I need to talk to you about something serious, and we need your help. Okay?" He waited until she gave a small nod. "Please know you're not in any trouble whatsoever, and this is just a friendly chat. You understand?"

Plum looked concerned.

"Some time ago, you used to work at the Flamingo Paradise. Correct?"

Plum lowered her eyes to the bare wooden floor. Grimble sensed a change in her attitude.

"Do you keep in contact with anyone who works or used to work there?"

"It was a long time ago."

"All we want is some information you might have, however small or unimportant it might be."

Plum gripped her knees and started to shake. Grimble had gone back to his soft, conciliatory tone but from her body language it was obvious to both policemen that she had shut down.

"I'm sorry if I've upset you, Plum, but it's important you talk to us. Do you understand?"

Grimble was greeted with what started out as a long wail and ended with sobbing. He looked to Cadd, who shrugged. They waited for some time on the sofa that reeked of cat piss, but Plum continued to cry. They kept their hands on their knees, a look of helplessness on their faces.

"Do you have a handkerchief, sergeant?" Grimble asked after a while.

Cadd took a pressed, white handkerchief out of his front pocket. He leaned over and held it in front of Plum's lowered face. She took it and started to wipe her eyes but continued to sob. Cadd looked at his boss, who in turn rose and straightened his trousers.

Plum was now wailing louder. She did not raise her head.

"I'm leaving my card here," Grimble said, still using his soft, conciliatory tone. "You can call me any time—and I do want to speak to Clovis."

She gave a small nod but continued to cry. The handkerchief was soaked.

"We'll see ourselves out."

Grimble stood by his Ford Falcon and faced Cadd, who shook his head and looked back at the house.

"What do you think?" Grimble asked as they drove away.

"Have you ever had anyone cry so much? Had me fooled for a few minutes. And she was shocked to see us, wasn't she. Recovered, though. Was that great acting?"

"Probably. Definitely the worst interview I've ever conducted. And there's something else going on there we don't know about. Did you sense that, Cadd?"

"Yes, sir. Was she on pills? Depressed? Something odd about her."

"If you're a professional violinist, it's my experience you're also a teacher. I didn't see any sign of pupils coming there. Did you?"

"What do you mean?"

"I only saw one music stand, nothing to indicate he's teaching. I've spent a lot of money on my daughter's violin lessons and seen a few studios. He does not teach there. So I wonder why? He would need the money. Playing in the orchestra can't pay that much. Should have asked her, but that crying put me off."

Cadd grinned. "And the smelly sofa, sir."

Grimble ignored him. When they reached Karangahape Road, he pointed to the other side of the street. "That's a strip club Terry Turner used to control, but it's no good going there now."

Cadd eyed the closed club as Grimble cruised past. "There's a rumor that Vice has their own table in the back."

"Ah, so you *have* heard something, sergeant?"

Cadd consulted his notebook. "Are we going to drive by Mrs. Turner's place?"

"Might as well—it's on our way to see your sergeant in Pukekohe. But you didn't answer my question about Vice."

"Just a rumor. Probably jealousy. Who doesn't want to sit in a strip club and get special treatment?"

"Really, Cadd," said Grimble disapprovingly.

.   .   .

Grimble pulled up beside the tall stone wall that enclosed the Turner property on a cul-de-sac in Epsom. The iron gates matched the wall in height and solidity. There were no cars parked in the driveway and the gate was locked. Well-trimmed hibiscus shrubs lined the driveway up to the house, and the lawn was immaculate and a deep green, despite the lack of rain.

"Doesn't look like anyone's at home, does it?" Cadd said.

Grimble frowned as he started the V8 engine. "Do you have any more insights to share, sergeant?" He gently tapped the accelerator and the motor roared.

Cadd kept his lips tight.

.   .   .

Dr. Mel Johnson walked into the empty reception area and saw that her last appointment for the day was late. The receptionist and the two other doctors who were on duty had already left. Her partners in the Ponsonby Women's Clinic were either at the hospital or making house calls.

The patient's name was not in the calendar and there was no file for the woman, Tiffany, who had phoned but left no details. Mel had a feeling she was about to meet another woman from a massage parlor who was reluctant to talk, despite her injuries.

Mel tied her long hair back and started to unbutton the white jacket she wore over a blue shirt when the front door opened and in walked a small, skinny young woman. She wore a long flowing black dress and her blond hair needed either a good combing or a wash or both. Mel introduced herself and led Tiffany into her office at the back of the clinic.

She offered Tiffany a seat and sat on a chair beside her rather than behind her desk.

"Now, Tiffany, how can I help you?" She noted that Tiffany had a slightly distended stomach, slouched shoulders and a particular body odor she recognized.

Tiffany kept her eyes lowered and took some time to reply. She kept her hands in her lap.

Mel waited.

"I've had some injuries," Tiffany managed to admit.

"Where?"

"Down here." Tiffany used one hand to point.

"And are you in pain?"

"Not really."

"Are you uncomfortable?"

"A little."

"When was the last time you had your period?"

"A couple of weeks ago."

"Do you practice birth control?"

"No."

"Do you have any discharge?"

"Oh. Sort of. But why?"

"You could have an infection."

"Oh, no. I douche regularly."

"That's not always a good idea. It can kill all the good bacteria you need down there. Do you have regular bowel movements?"

"Sometimes."

"What about now—are you regular?"

"I'm okay."

"Do you need to go?"

"No."

"Does it hurt when you urinate?"

"What?"

"When you pee?"

"No. I mean, I don't think so."

"Can I examine you?"

Tiffany shook her head. An emphatic no.

"Can I at least examine you, like this?" Mel knelt beside her patient and without waiting for a reply started to press one hand then the other over parts of Tiffany's abdomen through her dress, watching Tiffany's face for a reaction.

"Yes. That's where it hurts."

"What about here?"

"Not so much."

The examination lasted for another minute. "How did you get this?" she asked as she examined marks on Tiffany's left wrist, and then the right.

Tiffany withdrew her hands, folded her arms against her chest and tucked her legs under the chair.

Mel stood and walked to the chair behind her desk. "Tiffany, have you ever gone to the emergency department at Auckland Hospital or another doctor about this?"

"Yes."

"And what did they do?"

"They wanted me to have X-rays and file a report, but I didn't want to. I didn't want to lose my job."

"Where is your job?"

"I'm a masseuse."

"And where is that?"

"A place in Newmarket."

"You mean the Flamingo Paradise?"

"Yes, how did you know?"

Mel wrote on her pad *Prolapse? Recommend Kegel and biofeedback. Examine first.*

Mel looked at her patient. "Tiffany, I know this is difficult for you to answer, but I'm your doctor and I must ask you."

Mel waited for a response. There was none.

"Tiffany, has someone forced you to do something you didn't want to do?"

Tiffany kept her head down. "It's a good job. I get paid well and I get a car."

"You get a car?"

"Yes."

Mel thought for a moment. "Was this against your will? Did he rape you? Tie you up?"

Tiffany shook her head again. Mel had treated other women with related symptoms from the same massage parlor and they had a similar reaction—passive but frightened.

"Are you allergic to any antibiotics? Penicillin?"

"No, I don't think so."

"Then I'm going to prescribe some pills for you, take twice a day, with food and no alcohol. In ten days you should feel better. But I can't get you physiotherapy or biofeedback therapy until I examine you properly. Do you understand?"

Tiffany nodded but did not look up.

Mel stood and handed Tiffany a prescription. "There's a chemist on Ponsonby Road. You know it?"

Tiffany nodded again.

"I want you to come back in ten days. I can examine you and recommend some treatments. This can be fixed. You promise to come back? And I still don't have your full name and contact information for our records."

"Next time. I promise." Tiffany ran out of the office.

Mel heard the front door close. She sat in her chair for some time, chewing her pencil.

CHAPTER EIGHT

Hidden from the nearest paved road and further south from where Wiremu and Rawiri lived was a large wooden barn deep in the forest. Ancient kauri and totara trees still stood here, untouched by the early settlers' saws.

The barn was packed with the results of a successful harvest.

More than a year ago, Operation Weedout had been designed by the police to uproot illegal marijuana plots, transport the plants in nets to huge bonfires and destroy them. The story of the Huey helicopters the police had used to gather such large amounts of seized marijuana was still told among Wiremu's iwi, and how efficiently the flowering plants were dispersed so the airborne seeds could spread over Northland. Now a new generation of these government-assisted plants had grown to maturity.

Wiremu had split the harvest into two phases. By careful selection and curing on strings of rope tied between the walls of his barn, he had a large quantity of marijuana and clusters of buds he would store and sell separately. By the middle of February, after a wet spring and a dry summer, he had one load ready to be transported to Auckland and another to go further south. Big-volume dealers were desperate to replenish their stocks, and prices were rising because of the demand for their product. Then there was the panic over the shortages and the marijuana drought.

"Who's driving the truck?" Rawiri asked.

"Not you," Wiremu shot back, staring at his older brother. Roughly the same height, they looked like giants in their polished army boots, green pants and black woolen singlets. Rawiri had cut his hair as short as Wiremu's. Both had dark-brown, bloodshot eyes.

"I can," their cousin Moana said. She wore a red floral dress and sandals, her long dark hair tied in a ribbon.

Wiremu smiled at Moana. "We've come so far. I don't want to risk you, us."

"What? You're exercising restraint? Impulse control?" Moana shot back as she walked through the barn and ran her fingers lightly over the hanging plants.

"Are you studying psychology or something?"

"I can read. And I know a nephew who can do the run. Only we have to keep it between us."

Wiremu frowned. "Can he keep a secret?"

"Yes. And he has a driver's license too!"

Rawiri raised his eyebrows. "Well, aren't we all set?"

"Seriously. Half our iwi knows." Wiremu gestured to the rafters and the cured plants. "A lot of people have worked on the crop, but only *we* know about the transport. Even I don't know the details yet, cos I haven't worked it out. Is Ricky Wong still down for a few packages?"

"Yeah, but he wants to talk to you himself. Doesn't want to put me in the middle."

"Yeah. That's good." Wiremu stepped out into a beam of sunlight between two mature kauri trees. A piwakawaka was dancing in front of him, and he lost his smile as his eyes followed the small bird as it entered the barn. He shuddered. Last year the same type of bird had danced in front of him and he did not know what it meant. Now he knew.

Who will die this time?

CHAPTER NINE

When Police Commissioner Ian Thompson retired last December, Inspector Grimble thought he would never have to endure another clandestine meeting. But Thompson had booked a late-twilight special at the Point Chevalier golf course.

Grimble met him in the parking lot. "Get in my car," Thompson ordered. "No golf today."

Grimble eased into the dark green 1955 Riley Pathfinder.

"You like it? My son restored it. Thinks he's going to get it when I die. But I might just outlast British engineering."

"Nice leather, sir." Grimble kept quiet about the comb-over. The commissioner's thick silver hair had grown from one side to the other, almost hiding his bald head.

Thompson caught Grimble looking at it. "Whatever happened to your Honda?"

Grimble coughed into his fist. "Commissioner, I now drive a '72 Ford Falcon XA GT. Courtesy of our new Misuse of Drugs Act."

"Oh, yes. Well, with your work, you helped create the Act."

"The smuggler won't be needing his car anymore." Grimble glanced at the dark pine trees. There would be no tuis to mock him tonight. "It even has a blue light with a magnet, but no radio installed yet."

"Well, don't expect miracles. You're lucky to get the light. God, we should have sirens as well but the police are just another government bureaucracy sometimes. It's very annoying. Anyway, I didn't send for you to listen to me complain. What's going on now?"

"We surveilled the Looks. From nearby—we didn't go onto their property. I don't think we have reasonable grounds yet for a warrant, and I suspect they've already harvested their crop."

"What? Why didn't you inquire closer? This is unlike you, Grimble."

"Sir, I'm building something that'll stand up in court. I don't want to jeopardize the case with the sort of tactics the Drug Squad uses."

"We have the law on our side. What's come over you?"

"I want to be thorough. The Looks are only one piece of this complex puzzle. There's Terry Turner's wife, Barbara, then there's the Maori from Northland, Wiremu Wilson, and we don't know who else is involved. We have a drug conspiracy affecting the summer drought here in Auckland. I want to be careful but we're running out of time."

"It's February. Haven't the Chinese got their crop ready?"

"We think they're using new methods, but there are gaps in what we know. There's a lot we don't know."

"So what you're telling me is, you have collected enough to open a case. And if it leads to Barbara Turner and uncovers what she's doing, then we might only be one or two steps behind. But don't concentrate on her to the exclusion of everything else. I know you're not a cop who finds someone they like and then fits the evidence to convict the suspect."

Grimble kept looking at the tall pine trees.

"I've talked to Superintendent Jarvis several times, and he seems to think you won't find anything, but you already have."

Grimble scrunched his eyebrows.

"So do what you do best and bring in others if needed. The Minister has approved my role as unofficial guardian for the investigation. You can imagine how sensitive this is. We don't want any link to what happened before. You understand?"

Grimble stayed in his seat, unsure if the meeting had finished.

"What else have you been working on?"

"The body under the bridge. With no hands or head. Press have made a big deal of it."

"Oh yes. I remember the headlines. 'Headless in Herne Bay' and, my favorite, 'The Man Who Never Was.' Any progress?"

"Have you heard anything?" Grimble had always been amazed at how Thompson knew what was going on before he did, apart from his new requisitioned car.

"I'm retired now, remember."

"The body appeared by Curran Street, almost under the bridge. We still haven't identified him and no matching white male, twenty-five to thirty-five, has been reported missing."

Grimble shook his head. He had a hunch the body had been dumped near the bridge and the tides had pulled it back. The autopsy report had detailed extensive wounds to the body, including dislocated shoulders and multiple burn marks. What remained of the corpse's wrists showed extreme bruising and cuts. The medical examiner thought the burns were from a cattle prod and the body could have been suspended by the arms. Grimble had been shown stab wounds in the abdomen but they were not deep. Bacteria in the intact stomach and the upper intestines had caused the body to come to the surface after two or three days. He had interviewed fishermen nearby who confirmed the currents near the bridge could have pulled the body back once it had surfaced.

"Oh, and congratulations on your award, sir."

"Thank you. It's just as I said, an MBE suits me better than a knighthood. Without Alexander Newton, I wouldn't've got anything."

Grimble frowned. "You're not going to connect me with the curator again are you, sir?"

"Grimble, really. What do you have against him? Other than totaling your Honda? Without him you would be the one constable in some godforsaken town, getting beaten up every Saturday night by the local hoons. I'm glad you reminded me of him—he's going to Northland soon and talking on some maraes. We think he'll make contact with Wiremu Wilson."

When Grimble heard the name Wilson his eyes widened, and his lips curled into a smirk before he went back to his usual deadpan expression. He checked to make sure Thompson had not noticed.

"And he's been instructed to contact you for a debrief when he returns to Auckland. Wilson has revived his marijuana business, and we predict it'll be bigger than last year. The Minister's anxious leaders who are also drug dealers are brought to justice. Do you understand?"

"Yes, sir."

"I know now the war on drugs can never be won and will do more harm than good. You mark my words. It'll get worse." Thompson gazed through his windscreen as if he could see into the future.

"Well, sir, it's early days, isn't it?" Grimble suggested.

"Not the way I see it. Look at what's happening in prisons now. We're creating a new breed of criminal and nastier gangs. You can't tell me you haven't noticed?"

Grimble didn't respond.

"Anyway, get working on Barbara Turner," Thompson said. "Jarvis has been briefed. He will not be unhelpful."

.   .   .

The next morning Inspector Grimble was summoned to Superintendent Jarvis's office. He had to wait outside for twenty minutes until Jarvis's secretary let Grimble in.

"Inspector. Sorry to keep you waiting, but I was on the phone with the Commissioner, or rather former Commissioner Thompson, who had just spoken to the Minister. I wanted to keep you up to date so you know what's going on."

They shook hands and Jarvis pointed to a chair.

"Thank you, sir." Grimble sat opposite Jarvis and looked around his superior's office. Apart from a shelf of framed photos of the superintendent shaking hands with politicians, the mayor and visiting celebrities, the room was sparsely furnished. He was surprised to see a large color photograph of the Queen sitting on a horse, from her coronation day. He had never seen it in Jarvis's office before. The desk was bare but for a notepad, an in tray on one side of the glass-topped desk and an out tray on the other side. Grimble imagined that his immediate boss spent most of his day moving papers from one box to the other. The in tray was piled high with papers and files. The out tray was empty.

The superintendent leaned over his desk and fixed Grimble with his blue eyes. He was tall, thin and had a strong jaw. With his white hair cut short he looked a policeman's policeman in his perfectly pressed uniform, with his one pip and a crown insignia.

"The Minister is most concerned about this Wilson up north. Seems he has amassed another crop of marijuana and there are rumors he's going to bring it down here. I hear you have an inside man who can get to Wilson."

"Yes, sir." Grimble kept a straight face. He was not surprised Jarvis was giving him information he already knew. It was what he expected from his superintendent.

"We don't want any trouble, any shoot outs, any disturbances. You understand?"

"Yes, sir."

"For now we're not involving the Drug Squad. You understand?"

"Yes, sir."

"And what do I hear about Terry Turner's wife? Barbara Turner?"

"What about her, sir?"

"Well, forget her. It's preposterous to think a woman could run her husband's criminal empire. She's got nothing to do with it. Have you ever heard of a woman running something like that?"

"No, sir. I admit I haven't."

"Well, then, that's it. Now, have you made any progress on the headless man from the harbor?"

"No, sir." Grimble was loath to provide any additional information. His last report was probably sitting somewhere in the in tray. Jarvis had previously denied his request to share information about the body with Australian police.

"Well, work on that case. We can't have headless bodies showing up in Auckland. It might give other people ideas and before we know it, the harbor will be full of headless bodies floating about."

"Yes, sir." Grimble stood to leave.

CHAPTER TEN

"They're sitting on valuable land."

"What?"

"I mean the land could be subdivided for an entire new development. Lots of lovely houses, all the same. Where are those pot plants?" He squinted as he scanned the valley below them. The fields were full of neat lines of late-summer vegetables. "If you're thinking what I'm thinking, this is easier than flying to Oz again."

Barbara Turner handed the binoculars to Michael. "See the far greenhouse? Doesn't appear like anything is there. In fact, it's looks stripped."

"Harvested?" He adjusted the binoculars and let out a gasp. "They've harvested it already?" He kept the binoculars to his eyes. "Shit. Last time they were in full bud. Fuck. Where the fuck is it? They haven't shipped it, have they?" He lowered the binoculars.

"They have it somewhere, curing. Don't think they have it packaged yet," Barbara said. "We haven't heard from any of our dealers about any large movement. We would know."

Michael scanned the entire valley.

"What did our sergeant say?" Barbara asked.

"That greedy bugger in Pukekohe? He says he's keeping an eye on them. But I think he's shaking them down. I don't trust him."

"We pay him enough."

"Maybe we should tell the Looks what he's really doing. They could blackmail him."

"How? With a greenhouse full of sens all packaged?"

"But we're getting the crop."

"We are? How? And when were you going to tell me?"

His sister took the binoculars from him and surveyed the Looks' property.

They had parked on a ridge, and she could identify four greenhouses in the valley, a set of small buildings, rows of vegetables in neat lines as far as they could see, and a large ranch house at the end of a long driveway. Barbara spotted a Kawasaki motorbike next to a Volvo station wagon and a Ford Cortina.

"Chuck's new bike, Bruce's new car, and probably his wife's. He makes her drive an old Cortina. Cheap bastard." She lowered the binoculars and turned to her brother. "Did you know the body would float back to where you dropped it?"

"What? No, of course not. We never saw the last one, did we?"

When Barbara Turner screwed up her eyes her crow's feet were magnified.

"I dumped it right under the bridge and the tide was going out. What are the odds it would float back a few days later? Must be something weird with the current there. Anyway, with no face or fingers, they'll never figure out who it is. And I did burn all his clothes. Checked for tattoos. I was thorough. The idiot doesn't have any family here, so . . ."

"You didn't take any photos, did you?"

"No. Had too much to do. You would have said no anyway."

"You and your cameras. Christ. All we need, some photo book of yours and everything you've done falling into the wrong hands."

"Hey, I like live bodies. Like live young females. What do you think I am, a pervert?"

"Maybe the dolphins brought him back."

"What are you saying?"

"Dolphins. They save people who are drowning. Bev was telling me about this the other day. Saw it on the TV. They could have pushed him back to where he came from."

"Wouldn't that be Sydney?"

"Very funny. It's a better explanation than your current theory."

"Hah! You're making another joke?"

"Fuck, Mikey." Barbara stomped her right foot on the grass. "You were supposed to slit open the stomach. Otherwise the gases build and it comes to the surface. Shit! I thought you knew." She took a deep breath and turned away.

"Slit open his stomach? That's disgusting. Who do you take me for?"

His sister ignored his last comment but still gave him a dirty look. "Anyone asking about him at the club?"

"No."

"What, they're afraid of you?"

"Yes." He turned to his sister. "And what's with Bev? You haven't mentioned her in ages."

His sister squinted at him.

·   ·   ·

Barbara Turner drove back to Auckland lost in thought. Michael took a piece of rope he found under his seat, and started to practice his knots.

She braked next to her white Mercedes coupe in the Ellerslie car lot. "You're going to have to be careful, you know," she said.

"What do you mean?"

"What you do, Mikey. We've worked damn hard to build something here. Shit, in a few years we'll be completely legit."

"Legitimate? Remember, I manage all our businesses. I know what we do. We deal in heroin. Which is very profitable. I *know* what happens. Look at Oz."

"Mikey." His sister frowned as she looked at the knot he had tied. "What's wrong?"

"I drove past the Gold Club the other night. It was open at three-thirty. The numbers are down, by the way. I have no idea what's going on in the club after Oz disappeared. I need to visit more often. Keep a closer eye on things."

"I thought that's what you were doing. Maybe you should hang out at the club, get a decent girlfriend instead of all the toys you have at the Flamingo."

Michael cast a furtive look at his sister.

"Which reminds me," she continued, "what about the cameras in the Flamingo?"

"I'll install them tonight, with a hidden recorder. I think we can get something going there. Protection."

"Yes. And let me be clear about the girls. I've been hearing things. My dear, departed Terry used to say, don't ruin the merchandise. You know what I mean?"

Michael grinned and put the knotted rope in his pocket.

CHAPTER ELEVEN

Alexander Newton was summoned to Richard Catelin's office in the Government Building. Mavis, the secretary, ushered him into the huge room with its paintings, photographs of famous people, books, files and magazines piled high and the largest walnut desk Alexander had ever seen. Resplendent in a dark gray, double-breasted pinstripe, with a florid crimson tie, Catelin sat in his elevated leather armchair. Alexander chose the antique sofa. With his hands on his knees, Alexander admired his brown Italian loafers, his pressed navy-blue suit, solid dark-red tie and matching pocket square. He could hold his own with his boss when it came to style, he thought. All he needed now was a pipe, but he had never cared for smoking.

He watched the Permanent Under-Secretary of the Department of Internal Affairs go through the ritual of selecting a pipe from the rack on his large coffee table, filling it with aromatic tobacco, and producing thick clouds of smoke that rose to the high ceiling. Alexander glanced at the cocktail cabinet. There were no used glasses to be seen and no lingering presence of Old Spice, just the rich aroma of Catelin's latest imported Dutch tobacco.

"Is everything going okay with your scheduled visits this weekend?" Catelin asked.

"Yes. I talked to the director at the Arts Council and we're meeting at the Mangere marae, then I'm riding with him up north and spending Saturday night there."

"Has anyone briefed you about Maori etiquette, about being welcomed onto the marae, what to do, say, how to act?"

"Yes. I'm getting special tutoring." Alexander smiled. "Don't want to let the side down."

"Can't be too careful. They are very gracious but quick to be offended."

Catelin tamped his pipe with a small metal tool. White clouds encircled his goatee and wisps curled around his full head of dyed black hair.

"And while you're up there, I want you to search out Wiremu Wilson. He'll probably be at the one Ngapuhi marae you're all going to. It's the most important and he's a leader there. Get to know him, find out what he's doing. See if you can be invited to hang out with him. You'll know what to do. He's reputed to be the biggest pot grower in Northland and has a large group of people working for him. All family, iwi, local, loyal. We're on the lookout for any intelligence. Take your camera. You never know. Remember, you're a curator, not a spy. Inspector Grimble is involved and is anxious to be briefed by you once you return to Auckland. I presume you'll be staying a few extra days to sort things out." He smiled. "You have a new girlfriend, right?"

How did Catelin know about his girlfriend in Auckland? "Do I get a car or a van?" Alexander asked.

"Not necessary, but if you have to, rent one and take the insurance. Submit it to expenses. We'll reimburse you, if you don't crash."

Catelin stood and held out his hand. The meeting was over.

Alexander walked back to the National Art Gallery. He had plenty to think about.

CHAPTER TWELVE

Alexander sank into the large pillow and let out a sigh. A cool breeze wafted through an open window. He breathed in the scent of flowers from Mel's garden as he sweated. He saw the photo and poem he had sent her stuck on the mirror by her dresser and was reassured his presence was in her bedroom despite his absence. He held her as tightly as he could and was reminded how muscular her back and arms were, yet her skin was so soft.

Mel squeezed him back. "Tough going?"

"No. Just, I don't know, you seem different tonight."

Mel rested her head on his shoulder and played with his chest hairs. Something she had never done before. Alexander felt ill at ease. She focused on his torso, as if he was being examined. He could not tell what she was thinking.

On the last flight from Wellington, dressed in his navy suit and white shirt, he had a window seat on the west side, so he could take in Mount Egmont bathed in moonlight. He was reminded of the poster of Mount Fuji Deborah had in her bathroom. He recognized the stewardess who left the wicker basket in front of him a few seconds longer so he could select a second and third hard candy.

"Mr. Newton, we're so pleased you rescued Captain Cook. He's so important to our heritage. Well done."

Alexander felt on top of the world, even with an empty stomach, as he sucked on boiled sweets, and wondered how Mel would greet him. She had raced home, stripped off his clothes and they made frenzied love on top of her bed. Mel's long brown locks fell over his shoulders, and when she looked up he could see her amber eyes the color of gold. He felt he could sink through the mattress, she was so powerfully gorgeous.

"I've been thinking about this for weeks."

"It's been a while hasn't it?" Alexander felt exhilarated but guilty. He had dreamt of Mel for so long and now he was with her he should have been ecstatic, but the previous night he had been in bed with Deborah the librarian, or rather, he told himself, he had been learning about his Maori kawa.

Alexander had already told Mel about his itinerary on the drive to her house.

"I didn't know you spoke Maori."

"I don't, much. But I have index cards and have worked out what to begin with, the welcome, a little about my ancestry, what I do at the National Art Gallery, then our plan for the show I want to tour."

"And you think they're going to buy it?"

"I have no idea what will happen. That's the good thing about inexperience and naivety. You're never disappointed."

"You're not naïve. Not in my book." Mel rose on her elbow and gazed at him. Her breasts pushed into his chest and he sucked in his stomach, mindful he had not eaten since breakfast apart from the three boiled sweets. Her hand rested on his shoulder and he could feel the heat and the power of her fingers.

Alexander closed his eyes. "Well, we'll see, won't we."

"You should look for Wiremu Wilson while you're in Hokianga. He's a community leader and will probably be at the marae. Maybe he can help you."

Alexander opened his eyes and kept a straight face. "I need all the help I can get." He gazed at Mel's body. He stared at her nipples. Mel in turn scrutinized his body. He had very little body fat and his abs stood out, he knew.

Alexander's eyes wandered over her luscious lips, her patrician nose, her eyes, a muted amber, like a wolf's. Then he thought, wolves mate for life. What was he doing with another woman in Wellington? He could not shake his guilt.

Mel examined his eyes. "Are you seeing anyone in Wellington?"

Alexander could feel her breath. His heart stopped.

Alexander closed his eyes and breathed in her fragrance, then opened them to stare at her. What could he say without lying? Had she been monitoring his heartbeats? Was she reading his mind?

"I've been hanging out with someone, a librarian, but it's not serious, and I don't have the time or desire for it to be." He knew if he smiled he would give himself away, so he kept serious. He wondered if she could sense his heart start to race.

"How would you feel if I told you I was seeing someone here?"

"What? You are?" He rose on his elbows and almost knocked his chin against her forehead. He settled down and breathed out. "I would be jealous. Mad with jealousy. No, enraged with jealousy. Seething! Unconsolable! *Are* you seeing someone?"

"No. But you are. I don't think you're telling me the entire truth." She got off the bed and wrapped a red satin robe around her. She stood over him. "I think you should sleep on the sofa tonight. And you need to see a doctor tomorrow. I'll give you his number. He'll see you right away."

"I don't understand."

"No. You don't. And it's *in*consolable. Which I am, by the way. You could have told me before we, we . . ." She muttered over her shoulder, "I'm taking a shower and you can't join me. The blankets are in the hot water cupboard."

Alexander walked into the living room, where the weight of his emotions forced him to drop onto the sofa. His hair hung over his face and he buried his head in his hands. If he could have cried he would have emptied all the tears out of his body, but all he could do was clench his teeth and screw up his eyes until he saw stars, then complete darkness. He stayed immobile until he heard Mel return from the bathroom and shut her bedroom door.

When he opened his eyes he saw the large sound system and thought about playing Supertramp's *Crime of the Century*, but imagined Mel would storm in, turn the system off, and maybe hit him. Her violent physicality would be a consolation, for now he felt stupid and ignorant—or was it inconsiderate? He stretched out on the sofa and kept still as he gazed at a crack in the curtains where the streetlight seeped into the room. Why had he told her about Deborah? At least he hadn't mentioned her name.

Was sleeping in the living room for one night punishment enough? Would he be back in Mel's bed tomorrow or be thrown out of the house? He had hoped she would snuggle up to him or invite him back to her bed in the middle of the night. But the only certainty he could come to, after all his wishful fantasies, was how little he understood women. He was not as irresistible as he had thought.

Then there was the Deborah dilemma. What was he going to do about her? She was obviously an obstacle to his relationship with Mel. If he did not break up with Deborah he would lose Mel. If he did break up with Deborah, he had no idea how Deborah would react. He had been shocked to discover she knew about his spying. Would she blackmail him? Go to the newspapers? What exactly did she have over him? He felt vulnerable in his relationship with her; an unpredictable redhead. What he thought was an easy relationship had been exposed when she told him she knew he was photographing her neighbor, the doctor who had been tried and found not guilty in a sensational spy trial that gripped the nation. And all the time he thought he was fooling her. But it was the other way around, and he felt stupid.

Did Catelin know about Deborah? Or had he worked out where Alexander was staying from the photos? Had the SIS tipped off Catelin or were they working together? And what was the now cognizant librarian's relationship to his boss and the SIS?

Alexander thought back to the two empty whisky glasses and the lingering smell of Old Spice in his boss's office and the mysterious visitor who disappeared. What had Catelin warned him about months ago? He was one small piece in a larger operation and he had to follow orders. Catelin had stated there was more at stake than just his actions. Alexander was beginning to understand the implications now.

He switched gears and tried to imagine how Mel felt. Why would she have acted any differently to his betrayal? He was incapable of thinking about other people's feelings. A valuable trait when he had to focus on his mission, but when it came to personal relationships, he realized, his inability to put himself in the other person's shoes was a fatal flaw.

. . .

Alexander woke to the smell of coffee and stumbled into the kitchen wearing boxers and a shirt. Mel, in a red robe, was about to plunge her French press. He wanted to kiss her but feared she would attack him. He saw a large vase with dead red roses on the counter but before he could ask about them she pointed to the handwritten note on the kitchen table.

"Here's the phone number and name of the doctor. Mention my name and he'll see you right away." Alexander knew he could not approach her.

Mel appeared a moment later, dressed for work in a black trouser suit. Alexander was still in his underwear, drinking coffee.

"You'd better get dressed. I'm leaving now and so are you."

Alexander went back into the living room, found his trousers and shoes and returned to the kitchen. "Can I call you when I get back from Northland?" he asked meekly, unsure now where he stood with her, if he stood anywhere. "Please. We need to talk. I know I hurt you and I can't explain why it happened the way it did, but I need to talk to you. Please."

"Why? What do you think happened Alexander?" She glared at him and left no doubt as to her anger.

Alexander grabbed his bag, slung his suit jacket over his shoulder and faced Mel. He wanted to apologize, plead with her, but he was at a loss what to say. He turned on his heel and walked out of her house with a sense of dread their nascent relationship was over.

CHAPTER THIRTEEN

Alexander stood at the entrance to the marae in Mangere, next to the director of the Arts Council, Derek Sutton. Behind him stood several other people he had not seen before. He kept close to Derek as he witnessed his first powhiri, the formal welcoming ceremony onto the marae. He felt he was in another country.

To Alexander, Derek appeared like an oversized teddy bear with his straight, long sandy colored hair and light-colored suit. Derek always had an open smile, a warm handshake and he listened attentively to every word you said. Alexander thought the director managed to survive the small and difficult New Zealand art world by saying as little as possible and being polite to all, and he took note of the director's strategy.

Alexander wore a new dark-blue tie, a white shirt and his Italian loafers. He had his index cards in his inside suit pocket but had rehearsed his opening lines in Maori, so when it was his turn to speak in the meeting house, the wharenui, directly after Derek, he managed not to embarrass himself or the director.

He had left his camera in Derek's car, thinking it would be presumptuous to take photos without permission. As he had been instructed by Deborah, he followed a set routine which would have been the same as the speakers he had heard, if he had understood Maori. First he introduced himself and recited his memorized lines of greeting. He acknowledged the iwi, the tribal leaders who stood before him, then he explained his genealogy, where his ancestors had come from. He described his whakapapa, his family, as best as he could in Maori, and was able to compare his background with other speakers who had preceded him, not to show differences, but to demonstrate similarities.

Once Alexander had delivered his memorized lines, he switched to English and carefully laid out plans for a New Zealand touring exhibition of three leading Maori artists. He spoke their names and briefly described what they created. He explained how there would be special openings at each gallery in all the major cities where local Maori and Pakeha leaders would be invited, and he hoped for an extended dialogue about Maori art and its place in Maori and Pakeha society. He emphasized how art can heal divisions, reveal new possibilities in looking at the world. When he saw blank faces he stopped. He thought his speech had failed.

A tall man in an older, double-breasted suit stepped forward and addressed him. He spoke in Maori first and Alexander nodded until he realized he had no idea what the elder was saying. The look on Alexander's face must have been enough for the man to switch to English:

"What gives you the right to decide which Maori artists to show?"

"I have no right," Alexander shot back with a smile as he opened both his hands. "I'm just a curator with an idea for a show. I think these three artists are the best in their respective fields and are as good as any artists from any race, be it Maori or Pakeha. That they happen to be Maori I think enriches their art, the way they see the world and it shows in their works. I think it's important we acknowledge this, their talents and creativity. But it's not just cultural heritage, is it? There's a spiritual component as well." He paused as he looked at the elder, who stared back at him. "And we have to respect their spiritual integrity."

Another voice asked, "But why those artists? Aren't there others just as worthy?"

Alexander turned to face the whole audience. "Oh, yes. I would not for a minute claim these are the only three Maori artists we should celebrate, we should show."

Someone else stepped forward. "Why can't we select our own artists? Organize our own show? Tour it?"

"Sounds like a great idea. I would love to see such a show," Alexander said. "This is not about elite Pakeha art experts telling you what to see. You *should* be in control of your own art, your own culture. I hope the touring show is a catalyst for such thoughts."

Alexander was surprised at both the audience's reaction, brutally honest and assertive, and his measured responses. He understood that the verbal attacks were not personal—he was on their territory; he knew next to nothing about their culture. He listened carefully to what they said. Somehow his sincerity and openness in responding won over his vocal critics.

Later that night he found himself in his sleeping bag in the wharenui beside the director. They had their clothes rolled up next to them and the large space was full of people in sleeping bags, snoring or about to fall asleep.

The director turned to Alexander when it seemed most of the people around them were asleep. "You did good."

"Thanks. I was just following you, but I think I might have cost you another touring exhibit."

"Not to worry. We thought that would develop. Seems logical that if we fund your show, they should have their own tour with artists they select."

"Yes, what I thought happened tonight. We supply the logistics, the funding and they choose who they want to show at each marae. And I know just the guy to organize their tour."

"You?"

"No. I'll be busy with my three-artists show. I know a guy. I trained him, and he'll fit in with the relaxed atmosphere. He won't get flustered or upset if things don't go according to plan."

"I think I understand what you're saying. It's important to see the differences."

"You're driving north tomorrow, right?"

"That's the plan."

"And I'm riding with you?"

"That's the plan too. Good night."

Alexander lay on his back and looked at the dark ceiling. A group of young men were singing and playing guitars nearby. He realized he could not tell them to be quiet just because he wanted to sleep, so he took deep breaths and considered what Derek had said. His thoughts turned to Mel and how he could repair the damage, but he was too tired to think as he drifted off.

.   .   .

Derek the director and Alexander the curator left early Saturday morning for the long drive to Hokianga. Alexander thought the marae was near the harbor close to Rawene, but Derek had a map and instructions how to get there.

They drove to Dargaville and stopped for a burger on the main road. Acker Bilk was playing on the radio:

Midnight in Moscow. Alexander made slurpy noises with his passionfruit milkshake. He took photos of the shop and the main street. Back in Derek's rental car he commented on the Sixties feel to the place.

"More like the Fifties," Derek replied.

Alexander had forgotten how many shades of green there were in the countryside and how empty New Zealand was once you were out of the major cities or towns. A lone totara tree stood in the middle of a paddock surrounded by sheep. A fully loaded logging truck roared past them, followed by a milk tanker. Pukekos—tall, plump swamp hens—marched beside the road through swampland and there was a continual display of squashed opossums. In the distance he could see a harrier hawk gliding, its wings straight out, circling its prey somewhere ahead of their car.

By early afternoon they had made good time despite the narrow, empty and winding road as they passed through the Tutamoe Range and the Waipoua Forest. There were so many places Alexander wanted to stop to take in the scenery, the sheer majesty of their natural surroundings. He wanted to run along the sands of Baylys Beach, walk the track to the giant kauri trees including Tane Mahuta in Waipoua, and stop to admire the harbor at Omapere with its breathtaking views of the untamed Tasman Sea trying to invade the estuary, and the tall hills opposite, covered in sand, moving in the wind. But Derek was anxious to arrive early at the marae for the welcoming ceremony.

"They can be late. It's their schedule. But *we* can't," he explained, both hands on the steering wheel.

"The secret of your success?" Alexander asked.

"What, thinking of other people? I don't run a fiefdom. I'm a public servant."

Alexander nodded, and again decided to take a leaf out of Derek's book on how to survive in the art world. He would keep quiet.

.   .   .

Afterwards, whenever Alexander thought about his night in Hokianga with so many Ngapuhi, it felt like a dream. He had stepped into another world.

For a start, the powhiri was longer, more elaborate, and the haka fiercer than in Auckland. Derek added to his opening speech in Maori. Alexander would have panicked if he was the panicking sort, but instead he recited the same sentences Deborah the librarian had drilled into him. Then he did something different. He stepped forward and spoke from the heart. His suit was wrinkled and he had combed his hair with his fingers, but he stood to attention and addressed each person he looked at, moving from eyes to eyes until he came to a large, not-so-young man who just shone, his mana was so strong. He stopped his speech for a moment, took a deep breath, then continued as he realized that his unexpected break had sharpened the audience's attention. It was here, he thought later, that everything changed.

"I'm a curator at the National Art Gallery. I have an idea for a national tour of three contemporary Maori artists. I think they are extremely talented and at the top of their field. They need to be acknowledged for who they are. So many times in our short Pakeha art history we do not celebrate our local talent, whether they are Maori or Pakeha. These three artists will set a very high standard for emerging Maori and Pakeha talent. We need to honor and celebrate them now."

Alexander continued to describe the artists and how they were integrating their own culture, their painting and sculptural techniques with ancient Maori traditions, to make new exciting and challenging art.

"But don't for one minute think I am arrogant enough or stupid enough to think there are no other Maori artists worthy of such an exhibition or they are the best artists or there are no other Maori artists worthy of exhibiting in our Pakeha-dominated art galleries." He stopped and was relieved to hear laughter.

"No. There are many Maori artists out there who need to be shown, need to be introduced to the public, helped to grow as artists and that's why we're here to help.

"My show is going ahead anyway—we have the works, the funding, the galleries organized. I hope you will all come and see the show when it's here, I think in Whangarei, and Auckland. And the show will encourage young Maoris to become artists or be better artists.

"What has happened when we have talked on other maraes is that young Maori want to show their own work on their own marae and tour some of the work and show it to other iwis, on other maraes. So we've got to thinking, and I want to stress, and I can't stress this enough, I want to help you organize and tour your own travelling exhibition of Maori artists. We will help you with logistics, how to put it together and how to tour it, all the nuts and bolts of having a successful and professional show. But *you'll* be in charge of what's shown. *You* get to be the curators. *You* select who will be in your show. *You* get to be in control of your culture. Because what's more important than that? And the director of the Arts Council, Derek Sutton, has committed to funding and assisting with organizing the travelling exhibition." Alexander waved his arm toward Derek, who smiled.

There was loud applause. Alexander tried not to appear surprised.

He could not remember precisely what happened after. There was discussion, lots of discussion, but no heated arguments, no verbal sparring.

A large Maori with short, thick hair dressed in matching green army pants and shirt approached him once the meeting had finished. He introduced himself as Wiremu Wilson.

"Yes. Dr. Mel Johnson told me about you. I'm delighted to meet you." Alexander looked up to Wiremu, even though they were roughly the same height. Then he noticed a slightly older man next to Wiremu.

"My brother, Rawiri."

Alexander maintained his composure. "Delighted to meet you too. Mel said I would see you."

"Ah! Mel. How is she? Still doing her kung fu?" Wiremu asked.

Rawiri raised his eyebrows at Wiremu.

"Oh, yes," Alexander said. "Mel is . . . Well, she's very tough."

Rawiri and Wiremu exchanged looks again.

"Oh yes, she is tough," Wiremu said.

CHAPTER FOURTEEN

"The sink isn't going to fix itself."

Annie glanced back at Mel as they descended the wooden stairs from the borrowed dojo, a bare room with rubber mats above a boutique in a two-story wooden building. Mel had started Sunday morning self-defense classes by popular demand because her night classes were full.

Mel and Annie were both sore, but neither would admit it. Mel had been even more aggressive in their customary sparring session after the students had left. Annie was the perfect partner for Mel. She had a black belt in Okinawan karate, and trained for years in jiu-jitsu before embracing Mel's eclectic techniques. Annie was an emergency-department nurse at Auckland Hospital. Her long, wavy dark hair and creamy coffee-hued skin coupled with coal-colored eyes attracted male doctors—and a few nurses—whom she fended off verbally.

"The sensei who runs the place gives me free rein, so I can't complain." They were wearing track pants and T-shirts, still sweating in the late February heat. "He won't fight me, though. Seems to think that if I win, he'd have to give me the dojo. The last thing I want. Think he's watched too many old samurai films."

The boutique on the ground floor would open at noon, so there were no customers to complain about the noise and foot-falls coming from the creaky wooden floor above.

"Yeah. Why would you want it anyway?" Annie replied. "Time for coffee?"

"Dying for it and breakfast," Mel replied. "Usual place?"

"It's the only one open in walking distance."

They crossed Ponsonby Road and Annie had to grab Mel's hand as two cars came at them from the opposite direction. The row of shops they passed had changed as young professionals moved into Ponsonby Road around Mel's Women's Clinic. A copy-and-print business, an architect, a real-estate and surveyor firm, a pottery arts-and-crafts shop, and a coffee bar doing brisk business.

Mel broke into a tight grin as they ran to the other side of the road arm in arm. "Don't worry, I'm not going to do a flying kick into a windshield."

"Is there something you want to talk about?" Annie sat down with their two coffees. They had ordered a full breakfast at the counter. Annie placed Mel's coffee next to her own. "I've never seen you hit so hard and be ruthless in there. Something must be troubling you."

Mel held her coffee mug and eyed Annie over the steam.

"You keep your emotions close, don't you?" Annie filled the silence. "I know you confide in me sometimes, but I'm the only one, aren't I? But you need to beat the crap out of me first."

Mel laughed for the first time that morning. "Well, it's trust, isn't it. Trust is a big thing for me."

"I wonder why. What happened to you?"

Mel sighed. "Well, you're right. I need to talk and it seems you're the only one I can talk to." Her eyes started to tear. She took a deep breath. "I've no luck with men. I feel condemned to be single." She sipped her coffee. "The spinster doctor. Don't like the title." She held her cup to her lips and looked out at Ponsonby Road. "Is it so predictable that men cheat? Ah, here's breakfast."

The waitress delivered their plates and they fell on the eggs, toast, fried tomatoes and sausages. Annie checked the cap before she shook the tomato ketchup and poured a liberal amount over her sunny-side eggs.

"Still sore?" Mel asked after she had used the last piece of toast to soak the remains of an egg yolk and popped it into her mouth.

Annie finished her coffee. "Yes, I'm a little sore. After all, you took out all your frustrations on me, instead of whoever."

"Alexander."

"Oh. You never speak of him. What did he do? What caused you to go at me?"

"I'm sorry if I hurt you. Did I twist too hard the last time? You did tap out rather quickly."

"You were about to dislocate my shoulder and break my collarbone. I'm very attached to my clavicle. Both of them, in fact. The shoulder is the most complicated piece of engineering we have. You should see some of the rugby injuries we get on Saturdays."

"Do you work on Saturday at the emergency department?"

"Yes. Helps me keep my mind off previous boyfriends. But you're not over Alexander."

"I picked him up from the airport a couple of days ago. We made love. God, he's so good. I feel so right with him. You ever had the feeling you're so complete when you're with a man?"

Annie shook her head. "You are really in love with him, aren't you. I can tell by the way you hit me."

"I missed him so much and then, after we make love, which was fantastic, he confesses he's seeing someone in Wellington. A librarian. He's cheating on me with a librarian. How messed up is that?"

Annie took a deep breath. "A librarian?" She looked over to the counter. "We need more coffee."

.   .   .

"Are you going to welcome him back? What's to lose?" Annie said as they got to her Holden, a dull rusty color in need of a wash. "He might still redeem himself."

"You mean with my plan for the massage parlor? We talked about it last time, remember? Do you ever see workers from the Flamingo Paradise in the emergency department?"

"They don't say they work there, but we've had young women, walk-ins really, needing treatment. I thought they'd been raped but they insisted it was consensual and they wouldn't press charges. I know they work at a massage parlor but as soon as they're treated they disappear, as if they're afraid. The police aren't interested. So what do *you* have?"

Mel scanned the street. "They all have the same type of injuries. As if the same guy had attacked them but they were too scared to say or do anything."

"I remember one skinny girl recently. She was so pathetic. She said her name was Tiffany and she looked terrified when I mentioned the police and filing a rape report. She got dressed and ran out."

"Long blond hair, very skinny and about so high?" Mel held her hand to her shoulder.

"Yes, that's her. Why?"

"She came to me. It was obvious she was scared." Mel faced Annie again. "What can we do?"

"Well, at least you're teaching. Just be a little sensitive about your sparring partner next time. Perhaps you need to take it out on Alexander, not me."

"I just might."

Mel watched Annie get into her car and rev her engine. She wound down the side window. "Don't throw him away just yet. Despite my experience to the contrary, men can improve themselves, if given the chance." She winked at Mel, checked her mirror and roared off.

Mel stood on the sidewalk, her hands on her hips.

.   .   .

"Grimble hasn't got anything on us, you know. And he won't."

"How can you be so sure?"

"We have an in."

"We do?" Michael drove past what they thought was the house near Ponsonby Road. He was in a white van and checked both mirrors before he found a parking spot further along on the other side of the street where they could wait for her.

"I went to school with the superintendent's wife, Beverly Jarvis. You know Jarvis, the top cop, Grimble's boss?"

"Holy shit. You never cease to amaze me. You're telling me *that's* your Bev? The superintendent's wife? How long have you been consorting?"

"Forever. And do you know what consorting means?"

"Do you?" he shot back.

"Besides, we're very respectable, co-chairs of the fundraising committee for our tennis club. We raise a lot of money for the poor kids. We are Babs and Bev when we play doubles at the club. And we are unbeatable."

"She knows who you are?"

"She tells me everything."

"But does she *really* know who you are?"

"I'm queen of the underworld. Of course she fucking knows who I am—and she loves me for it."

Michael rolled his eyes.

"Come on, Mikey. Not every women who has solidarity with another is a lesbian."

He gave a wry smile.

"I saw that, Mikey."

"Then why are we checking out this girl?"

"She helped kill my husband." Barbara took a deep breath then whispered, "And she has to pay."

"And you were going to tell me when?"

"I'm telling you now. Shit, a lady's got to have some secrets. Besides, vengeance is mine."

"Are you quoting Shakespeare?"

"Fuck Shakespeare. I am feared by everyone who knows me."

Michael kept quiet as he surveyed Ponsonby Road and the surrounding streets with his side mirrors. "This area has come up, hasn't it?"

"What do you mean?"

"Never thought it would amount to much with all these small, old cottages but it's a busy place now."

"You're thinking of buying here?"

"Yeah. A few properties we can get on the cheap. The renters will fix them for free. It would be an investment."

"What about collecting the rent?"

"Leave it to me."

"And if they fall behind, what are you going to do? Beat the guy or seduce the girl?"

"Seduce?" Michael turned to his sister with a quick grin. If Barbara had a catalog of nasty looks she threw at her brother, the one she gave him now would count as the worst.

"Do you see her?" Michael leaned over the steering wheel and started the van.

"There she is. Don't lose her."

"No worries. She's walking home with groceries."

Michael made a U-turn and pulled into the curb to watch a young woman with an overgrown pageboy haircut and dressed in a red plaid skirt turn down Lincoln Street. He followed her in the white van.

Barbara eagerly leaned forward, excited to finally catch sight of her prey on their second attempt to locate Plum Blossom.

Michael glanced at his sister. "I heard the rumors."

"What rumors?"

"She was Terry's bit on the side. She worked at the Flamingo, right?"

Barbara scowled before fixing her eyes back on the young woman, who entered a small, one-story wooden house, a few doors from where they had parked.

"Why are we here? What's the point? I could be in my office making money."

"It's not all about money, Mikey. She's responsible for my husband's demise. Besides, it's Sunday. Would you rather be watching young men in tight shorts playing rugby and biting each other's ears? Now we know where she lives."

"You're not planning something, are you?" Michael scrutinized his sister's face. The creases on her forehead, her crow's feet, her thin cruel lips. "Do you want me to do her now? You brought the van. And you're sure her boyfriend is at rehearsal, right?"

CHAPTER FIFTEEN

Alexander said goodbye to Derek after a community breakfast at the marae. He had slept poorly in the early hours of Sunday morning. He had drunk too much beer the night before, then he had to find the latrine outside in the dark, before locating his sleeping bag again in the dark wharenui. To make matters worse, he had again been kept awake by young men who sang songs and played guitars until four in the morning. He could not decide whether he liked badly sung reggae more or less than a competent rendition of *Ten Guitars*.

Wiremu met Alexander at the marae, and took him in his rusted cream-colored 1966 Holden Special sedan to his friend Bill, a traditional carver. Bill took Alexander out the back to a workshop in his garden. The entire backyard was full of large upright logs waiting to be carved. Inside the open workshop was a large, free-standing kauri post. Bill explained that Wiremu had found it in a swamp. Along the corrugated-iron walls were several poupous, wood panels he was working on. A bench contained various sizes of adzes, the chisel tools he used to carve the detail in the wood.

"Every piece of wood tells a story and I have to bring it out," Bill stated, putting his beer bottle down and grabbing an adze. "Wiremu's post is going to be a pouwhenua. We're going to place it in a special place. It's Makeatutara, guardian of the underworld and father of Maui." He winked at Alexander, and grabbed his beer again. He clearly assumed that Alexander would understand the references.

Alexander followed Bill back to the living room and listened intently as he and Wiremu discussed the carvings. Despite the four beers and lack of sleep, Alexander was beginning to gain a new respect for the fine art of traditional carving. Like visiting a painter's studio and seeing works in progress and finished pieces, he appreciated the thought, technique and storytelling involved in a very old art form so different from the European-influenced sculpture he had seen in Pakeha artists' workshops.

Back in the car, Alexander sensed that Wiremu and Rawiri had something up their sleeve, but he did too, so he kept quiet. They had stopped at the local pub and he bought them first a glass of lager and then they walked around the back of the pub and Alexander bought a crate of beer. He was unsure if the off-license was open or closed, but it was Hokianga so he assumed they were operating under their own rules.

He carried the crate to the car and admired the view of the harbor on the short trip to the house. The stretch of water was devoid of boats. The rolling hills opposite looked as if they had been painted with thick brush strokes. The air was heavy with dust and humidity but fragrant from the smell of manuka. Alexander still wore his white long-sleeved shirt from yesterday—the brothers looked comfortable in their black woolen singlets.

Before long Alexander was in the back seat with his overnight bag and camera, his eyes fixed on Wiremu who parked the Holden on the grass next to his house. The Victorian villa was similar in style to Mel's in Mount

Eden, but in need of some paint and some repairs. A *lot* of paint and repairs, Alexander thought, as he admired the wooden fretwork and other ornamental elements around the veranda and the bay window.

He left his bag by the front door, unsure where he would sleep that night. He carried the crate of beer into the house then followed the brothers, still holding his crate, to a paddock by the beach where they set blankets and a few plates and utensils from the house.

The tide was coming in as Alexander stood on sand, his camera slung over his shoulder. A fire was tended by a young woman in a red floral dress, with long dark hair, wide-set eyes and a straight nose. She looked as if she had stepped out of a painting. Alexander kept this thought to himself.

"Moana, Alexander Newton," Wiremu said. "Our new friend from Wellington. He's organizing the Maori art touring show and spoke at the marae last night."

"Yeah, I recognize you. Hi." Moana had her hands full of manuka sticks she was feeding into the fire. She squatted by a bucket of mussels. She placed a metal grill with pipis over the embers, their shells already open.

Alexander gazed at the estuary and the hills opposite. He was reminded of a famous landscape painter, but could not think of his name. At the shoreline he adjusted the aperture and focus to obtain as much depth of field as he could using the existing light. He composed shots of the hills and the harbor with his Nikon. He peeked behind him and saw they were preoccupied with the fire and the mussels. Without turning around, he clicked a few photos of the three. In the quiet the shutter sounded like breaking glass. They ignored him.

He lifted his head to see a harrier hawk glide along thermals, adjusting its wings to change direction. He tried to capture its flight with his telephoto lens but without success, and he wished he had Mel with him to share this experience, being at the water's edge at the end of the day.

He sat on a blanket, careful to have his camera pointed away with the lens cap on. "It's magical," he said.

"Yeah," Wiremu let out. "Gets better after a few beers and a belly full of mussels, eh?"

Rawiri and Moana laughed.

Alexander watched Moana place the mussels over the fire and poke the glowing embers. She turned and stared at him. He felt uncomfortable. All he wanted to do was to take his camera and shoot what he saw: Moana's face illuminated as she knelt by the fire, the expanse of water, a deep flat blue, and the silent darkening hills behind her.

.   .   .

They sat in a circle on the blankets and ate the pipis and mussels Moana had cooked. The brothers seemed to groan after each mouthful. The sky had turned to purple and there were dark pink streaks of clouds painted over the hills. The light was a rich gold. After the second bottle of beer Alexander turned to Wiremu. "Is that pounamu around your neck?"

"Yeah."

He was tempted to lean over and inspect it. But he thought better of such an action, and Moana kept glancing at him in a strange way. He took his camera from the blanket so they could see it.

"Is it okay to take some photos? The light is fading, and I have to take them now."

Wiremu looked curiously at Rawiri, who turned to Moana. Alexander was unsure how they would react. He dared not take photos of them openly.

"Why don't you take some tomorrow morning?" Wiremu said softly. "Better light."

Alexander nodded, placed the lens cap back and put his camera in its bag, closing the bag's zip with a flourish, aware that the three were watching him.

Wiremu exhaled loudly. "At the marae you said you have a patronymic. Why?"

Alexander frowned. "Yes."

"Everyone reads *Crime and Punishment* in Parry. We love Dostoevsky."

"I thought I had to establish my ancestry. My grandfather was Russian. My full name is Alexander Arkadyevich Newton."

"Yeah, I liked your introduction. The whole Russian thing at the marae set you apart."

"My father named me after Alexander Pushkin, the great, some say the greatest, Russian writer, but I never saw him read a book.

"Pushkin? Didn't he die in a duel?"

"Yes. When he was thirty-seven. His brother-in-law shot him."

Wiremu laughed. "My kind of guy."

"The brother-in-law?" Rawiri grimaced.

Wiremu shook his head.

"What happened to your mother?" Moana asked. "Are you in contact with her?"

"No. I have no idea where she is or even if she's alive. So I'm English in name but Russian in my blood. I feel at times like two different people. What about you?"

Moana glanced at Wiremu and Rawiri for support. Alexander leaned back to gaze at the stars, but it became obvious no one was going to respond to him.

"Wiremu, I noticed you had bear claws hanging in your hallway. I heard a relative of mine, I have no idea of his name, had a plan to bring Russian bears to New Zealand but I could never find out what happened to him or if the bears even existed. I thought it was another of my father's tall tales."

"Oh, they existed. They existed all right," Wiremu said. "In 1885 a Russian ship came to Lyttelton. It caused a sensation at the time because the Pakeha thought they were going to be invaded by the Russians. Kinda funny at the time, really, as *they* had invaded *us*. The Russian had two bear cubs but one died during the voyage over. The Russian eventually came to the Bay of Islands in about 1888. He visited our iwi and stayed. He drowned fishing. He couldn't swim. My great-grandfather, who was a tohunga, took to the bear. It slept in a special hut next to him. It would follow him everywhere. Then one day the bear attacked him. Both were tapu. You could not touch them, but the tohunga could stroke the bear. The bear loved having his thick brown hair combed."

"What happened to your great-grandfather?" Alexander asked.

"He killed the bear and ate it. Those are the bear claws on the wall to remind us."

Alexander finished his third beer, thought for a moment and said, "A beautiful story. But you don't wear the bear claws around your neck."

"Have you seen those claws?" Wiremu was deadpan for a few seconds then burst out laughing. Rawiri and Moana joined in.

"Talking of powerful, do you have anything stronger?" Alexander asked.

Eyeing Wiremu, Moana reached into a pocket in her dress.

"Guess it's time to try some local gold," Wiremu whispered.

Moana produced a tobacco pouch and a fat reefer appeared. She lit it, inhaled, and held the smoke in with her eyes closed before passing the joint to Wiremu, who repeated the ritual and passed it to Rawiri, then Alexander. He sucked on the roach until his fingers were burnt and smoke seeped into his lungs. He wanted to cough but dared not. They watched him as his eyes bulged before he let out his breath. "Some serious strong shit. Wow."

Alexander hoped his vocabulary was appropriate, although he had lost his reason, his sense of where he was, and perhaps who he was. The others laughed, which he took to be a good sign. He had passed their first test—or was it their last? The harbor was now silver-gray, iridescent, and he wished he could capture the moonlight on his Tri-X fast film and solarize the black-and-white prints. Instead he was oscillating between paranoia and stoned ecstasy.

"So we're kind of related then, with the bear and my great-great-uncle who came to your iwi," he said after a long silence. "Is he buried nearby?"

He felt uneasy as they stared at him. He had discovered what had happened to the long-lost relative he never knew he had, but had he crossed an unseen line when he asked what had happened to the Russian's body?

.   .   .

Speakers hung from the rafters; big wooden boxes with twelve-inch speakers. He had never heard Jimi Hendrix playing *Purple Haze* sound so alive. The sound and smell was overwhelming. Alexander wore his denim jacket over his white shirt, even though it was hot inside the large barn. Using his left hand only and with his compact point-and-shoot Rollei 35 hidden in his left front pocket, he managed to squeeze the shutter of the camera and flicked the winder back as many times as he dared. He lost count of how many photos he had taken.

When the song finished he turned to look for his host, who had wandered off between the racks of drying plants. Wiremu returned to his side and for a moment Alexander thought he had been caught.

"An amazing place," Alexander smiled as he surveyed the rafters. On the opposite wall were what looked like large jars of dried marijuana and piles of cardboard boxes. Alexander thought there was another person behind the boxes. He saw a figure hold an album and take out the record.

Wiremu snorted and squinted at Alexander, standing close to him. "You said you could take at least five pounds."

"Maybe more. I have contacts in the art world. Everyone loves to smoke weed. Not me. As you can tell. Strong stuff last night. I'm still stoned. I'll stick to Southern Comfort, thank you."

Wiremu grinned. "Beer works for me."

"By the crate." Alexander smiled to mask his nervousness. "When can I get the stuff?"

"We'll contact you when we're ready. But can you help drive my car tomorrow to Auckland? You staying at Mel's?"

"Yes. Why?" Alexander felt he had missed something.

"Good. Drop the car off at Mel's. You got her phone number?" Wiremu smiled. "Give it to me." There was a loud clang of a cowbell as Jimi Hendrix started *Stone Free*.

Alexander walked through the large double doors of the barn into the fresh air of the forest. Away from the music, the birds were singing, the wind rustled through the trees and sunlight made shadows on the grass. Everything seemed so bright and vivid. He turned to Wiremu and asked a question that no one who was an informer or an undercover cop, he thought, would dare ask.

"What made you trust me? This is a huge operation."

"You're with Mel. She saved my life and I trust her. Therefore I trust you. And there is the bear—as you said, we're almost related. It's important. Family. Iwi."

Wiremu looked him in the eyes. "For now."

CHAPTER SIXTEEN

Barbara Turner had opened her iron gates so that when the taxi arrived her guest could walk up the driveway to the Victorian-built stone house. Barbara stood by the two Mercedes coupes parked next to the front steps.

"Oh my! That is beautiful." Beverly Jarvis put her hands to her mouth and her eyes filled with tears.

Barbara held the keys for her and noticed they had matching hot pink nail polish. She wore a red silk pant suit with a plunging neckline, full Cleopatra eye-make-up and her long black hair was teased out.

"It's yours. All checked out. I got everything serviced. 1972 Mercedes-Benz 350 SL. Fit for a princess."

"I love the color."

"Silver, the color of money."

Beverly tried to frown. "Not gold?" Even in flat tennis shoes she stood taller than Barbara, wearing a white T-shirt and tiny shorts to show off her perfectly tanned long legs. They both had fake eyelashes.

"Didn't want you to be too flashy, you know?"

They chuckled together.

"It's got its original hardtop installed but I'll show you later how to change it. Will make quite a splash at the tennis club."

"Won't it. Wonder what my husband will say?" Beverly adjusted the pink head band to keep her long blond hair in place.

"You can tell him anything. He'll believe you."

"Ain't that the truth." Beverly shook her head. "He's playing golf this afternoon, won't miss me at all."

"Do you regret marrying an older man, Bev?"

"I didn't want children. He gives me security and he's the top cop. What could go wrong?"

"Like your marriage?"

Beverly looked at Barbara under her long eyelashes. "I have you."

"Get in the car."

Beverly opened the door and eased into the cream leather seat. Barbara walked around and sat in the passenger seat. Beverly clutched the steering wheel with both hands, her eyes wide. Then she pulled down the visor and saw the small mirror. She checked her face and make-up.

"Start it up."

Beverly grasped the gear stick firmly with her left hand and grinned at Barbara as she checked it was in neutral. Barbara returned the look. Beverly turned the ignition and the car came alive. She gently tapped the accelerator and the engine revved. She listened to the engine as it idled. "Sounds perfect. Shall we go for a drive?"

"Tank's full."

"You haven't locked your door?"

Barbara grinned. "No one's going to break into *my* house."

"That's my Babs."

"Goodness, look at the lace curtains flapping. I can hear the neighbors gossiping already."

Beverly changed into second before stopping at the end of the street. She expertly worked the clutch as she slid through the gears and headed toward Gillies Avenue and onto Khyber Pass Road.

"Did he tell you what he's working on now?" Barbara asked.

"Well, he stopped the investigation. The one you asked about. Was the information about Plum Blossom helpful?"

"Oh yes."

"You know he keeps on about his inspector, what's his name?"

"Grimble."

"Yes, Grimble. He can't stop talking about him. Like Grimble's undermining his authority, Grimble's going cowboy. I think it's his favorite expression. You'd think with his looks and build he wouldn't be so insecure. He's like a little boy sometimes, but he tells me everything."

"Like what?"

"Well, there's a huge shipment of pot coming down from the north, you know, like last time. Maoris. And they're watching out for it."

Barbara nodded thoughtfully. "What about down south. Hear anything about the Chinese?"

"Yes, come to think of it. You know he does go on about certain things but he only mentioned, who are they? The Looks, once. How could I forget such a name? Something about they're harvesting some kind of super-strong pot but my genius husband doesn't know where it all is, which I find hard to believe."

Barbara chuckled. "You said it."

"Or maybe he said they didn't have enough for a search warrant. It's hard to keep track of everything he goes on about. I doubt he knows what he's talking about either, half the time."

They both laughed as Beverly turned back on to Mountain Road to the house.

"I've made margaritas," Barbara said. "The way you like them. Cointreau, fresh limes and the tequila I brought back from Sydney."

"Then what are we waiting for?"

"Hey, don't speed down my street."

Beverly laughed as she slowed and turned into the driveway and parked in front of Barbara's white coupe.

"Come inside. We need to celebrate."

"Can't wait." Beverly adjusted her white head band again and her eyes followed Barbara's rear as she walked into her house. Barbara turned around when she sensed Beverly's eyes on her, and gave a little smile.

In the kitchen she took a large jug of margaritas from the refrigerator. She ground the top of the glasses into a ring of specially prepared salt and poured two drinks. Then she made a show of handing one to Beverly.

"You look very nice in those shorts, Bev." She held her drink as she stood very close, with one hand on her friend's shorts. Her hand moved from the side to the rear and squeezed.

"And you look stunning in your outfit." Beverly moved her hips as she pressed against Barbara. She took a sip of her drink, licked the salt from her lips, moaned and closed her eyes.

CHAPTER SEVENTEEN

Alexander made an appointment with Mel's doctor from a phone box in Orewa. He was the last patient of the day when he reached the Mount Eden clinic, set behind a volcanic rock wall, a large, two-story Victorian wooden house. The doctor, in a white coat and a Beatles mop haircut, asked Alexander to strip and carefully examined him with rubber gloves, as if he was some strange new species. Alexander wanted to make a joke, but thought the doctor was probably devoid of humor and anything he said would be reported to Mel, so he kept quiet, answered the doctor's questions and when told to, bent over, breathed in and out, and coughed with the minimum of fuss.

Afterwards he drove to Mel's dojo. It was Tuesday night so she would be conducting her class, and he thought he had a better chance of her accepting him there, in front of witnesses. He would have to volunteer to play the male attacker. Perhaps if she beat him up in front of her students she would feel he had atoned for his behavior in Wellington.

When he parked, he took a moment to survey the street in the evening rush hour. He was struck by how different the light was to Wellington's, with the setting sun and the humidity giving way to a cool breeze. He imagined living here again if he could find a job in a gallery and make a life for himself with Mel. If he could repair their relationship.

.   .   .

Mel was taking her students through a vigorous warm-up followed by stretching and basic body-weight exercises. The routines were very similar to what he had started in Wellington to get back into shape, his XBX plan, from a book he had found in a secondhand bookstore on Cuba Street. He placed his shoes and socks next to the other shoes at the entrance.

She introduced him to her fifteen students, including Annie, whom he acknowledged with a bow. Alexander was invited into the circle where Mel instructed him to grab her from behind. He was careful with his slow deliberate movements as he used both hands to grab her around the waist. He tried to pick her up and was not sure if she expected him to do such a move.

Before he could lift her off her feet Alexander found himself on the floor. He heard the women in the circle laughing then Mel's face came into view.

"Are you okay?" she asked.

"Only my ego is damaged. What happened?"

"Here." She extended her left hand and pulled him to his feet. "Let's go through this slowly. What is it we say? Slow is fast, fast is smooth. Here, do it again. Grab me from behind."

Alexander was hesitant to go near her. "You're not going to throw me again, are you?" More laughter from the attentive audience.

"Just put your hands here." Mel guided his hands around her narrow waist. She bent her knees, grabbed his left ankle between her legs with both her hands and pulled. It looked very easy as Alexander went splat on the ground and Mel spun around, ready to stomp on his middle region. He remembered at the last moment to shoot his arms out and slap the mat, stop his head from hitting the floor, and not bite his tongue.

Alexander stayed on the floor, and slowly lifted his head to check that he still had his vital parts intact. The audience looked concerned.

"That was not what I wanted to show you. Here." Mel extended her hand to him again. "But you have to use whatever comes to mind. You can't stop and think, what should I do now? It doesn't work like that. Be aggressive, fight back. Surprise. Speed of action."

This is exactly what I feared would happen, Alexander thought. *I was shagging a librarian and now I'm getting the crap beaten out of me by a kung-fu doctor. Am I earning redemption or is she just taking her frustration out on me?* Deservedly, Alexander admitted to himself, as he smiled at her and nodded. "Again?"

"Please. Now I'll go slowly."

Alexander knew better than to make a smart remark. He walked behind her and grabbed both her elbows. With no martial-arts experience, he had no memory of how he moved before, so grabbing her elbows instead of putting his arms around her waist seemed logical to him. Mel eased her left foot back, twisted her body and, when Alexander tried to adjust to her movements, used her right hand to grab his left wrist. She kept moving to her left then, once her left hand wrapped around his right wrist, she changed direction. Instead of continuing in her spinning motion she went in the opposite direction, bent his wrist backwards and he lost his balance. Under her controlling wrist-lock he fell to the mat, using his right hand to break his fall.

"Now I did this slowly, but all I'm doing is making him lose his balance, gaining control of one hand and putting him on the ground. When it's done faster, the attacker is thrown to the ground, and gets his wrist and maybe his arm broken. It's a nasty move, so please be careful with your partner. Remember, slow and smooth. We all want to walk out of here in one piece."

More laughter. Alexander tried to laugh as well, but his butt was sore and he knew she had not finished with him yet.

"Now let's go through it again. Remember we do drills and do them till we can execute them automatically. Over and over. Without thinking."

Mel turned to Alexander and motioned for him to grab her again from the rear. Alexander hesitated, unsure whether to grab her elbows or her waist.

.   .   .

Annie and Mel waited for the students to leave before they began their sparring session. Alexander watched from the window seat and noted how Annie handled Mel's attacks. Afterwards, he followed them down the steps to the street. They did not change their clothes but had used towels to dry themselves.

Alexander was introduced to Annie again. He suspected the two women wanted to be together to talk, but Annie kept quiet and gave Mel a look he could not interpret. Mel asked when he had arrived, and he told her he had just driven from Hokianga. When Annie excused herself, Mel turned to Alexander who offered to take her to a restaurant in Parnell.

As he followed her BMW there he recalled his moment of clarity stretched out on the grass in Hokianga Harbor, watching meteors shoot across the sky, stoned from his first sample of local weed. He wanted to be with Mel. He had never been in love before and these emotions were confusing to him. He was so consumed with these thoughts that he almost rear-ended her when she came to a stop at the traffic light at the Broadway intersection.

They had a quiet but tense meal in an Italian restaurant. Alexander wondered how she had managed to change and look so effortlessly beautiful in a trouser suit, when she had been dripping with sweat in loose pants and a T-shirt in her dojo.

He briefly mentioned his talk at the marae and how he met Wiremu. He omitted the events of the next day and his tour of their secret facility. He kept asking her questions about her training at Otago Medical School, her practice, whether she liked working there, what the other women doctors were like, what her plans for the future were, if she saw her parents often. He wanted to keep attention centered on her. So it was a relief, once he had paid, that Mel asked if he wanted to come back for a drink.

He accepted and found himself sitting on the floor, thumbing through her albums, while she prepared a pot of tea. He was anxious for a physical reconciliation and tried to mask his feelings by waving an old album.

"You bought the Small Faces?"

"Yes. One of my favorites."

"Why? It's, what, ten years old?" Alexander pressed his hands to the floor and got up. His left knee hurt, and his kidneys were sore. He had already passed blood in her bathroom. Maybe he could play the sympathy angle later but for now he was intrigued, and he forgot his pain.

"I'm glad I never went for the Small Faces look with their Mod haircuts." He ran his hands through his hair, annoyed that Mel had not commented on his dojo participation or his evident pain.

"And this is relevant because?"

Alexander looked at her feet to see if she was going to dance or launch a roundhouse kick.

"Hmmm. I don't know. Just curious. I want to know all about you, but you keep your cards close to your chest. Talking of which."

"Oh, no." Mel was dancing to *I Feel Much Better*. She put her hands up to stop Alexander's advances. He had to be content to dance next to her, and watch her enjoy the music. He wondered how he could unlock her majestic remoteness. How could he win her back?

She stopped and walked into the kitchen to put the kettle on again. Alexander followed, unsure of his role. He had left his bag at the front door.

"I got tested earlier."

"Yes. The doctor phoned. Seems you are okay, for now."

"That's a relief. I wondered what I could have contracted."

"You'd be surprised." Mel spooned Darjeeling tea into a plain white tea pot then poured in the boiling water. She placed two mugs on the counter and looked at Alexander who sat by the small table in the kitchen. Again he noticed the dead red roses in a vase on the counter. He had ordered the roses three weeks ago.

"You were going to tell me about Inspector Grimble. The last time I mentioned him you pulled a face. And you never pull faces. He upsets you?"

"God, you're starting to know me," Mel muttered.

"Such a bad thing, to know you?"

"No. But you never explained about the woman you're seeing in Wellington."

"Oh. Technically she's teaching me Maori and kawa, and she's part-Maori, so it's business. Besides, you didn't want me to make a fool of myself, did you? And you're avoiding the question about Grimble."

Mel poured him a cup. "You don't take milk or sugar, right?"

"Yes. And what about my mate Grimble? Why was he so special to you?"

"He's your mate now? Anyway, questions later. What I want you to think about is the Flamingo Paradise. It's a massage parlor in Newmarket and young women are coming into the clinic with, let's say, some injuries. They won't go to the police, and I can't tell you who they are, but something's not right. I need to know what's really going on there. "

"It's a massage parlor." Alexander stopped before he said anything else to annoy her. He could see how intense and serious she was.

"I've treated women from there and the strip club on K Road since we opened, but this is different. You need to visit, probably a few times, and find out what's going on. Late at night would be good. And just so you know, Moana worked there too. Wiremu's niece."

"Ah, Moana." Alexander wondered what else she was not telling him.

Mel finished her tea and placed the mug in the sink. She stared at Alexander who kept sipping his tea, stalling for time.

"Let me be clear here," he said. "You want me to go to a massage parlor, chat up the girls, do some surveillance, and find out what's going on?"

"But no funny stuff or specials or whatever they call it."

"Phew. When do I start?" Alexander put the mug down. "I need to know more. Who owns it, its hours and so on. I'll need a car."

"You have a car out there."

"But I can't use it here. Wiremu's going to retrieve it, or someone is. I drove it down so I could be with you."

Mel kept quiet. Alexander wanted to ask what was going to happen tonight. He was too tired to go to the Flamingo Paradise now. He had been driving all day and all he wanted to do was lie on her bed and hold her. Just to cuddle her would be heaven, but it was not going to happen.

"Then you'll do it?" she said at last.

"Of course. I'm your jaded spy. Remember?" He wanted to kiss her, but knew it would be the wrong move.

"Good. You can sleep on the sofa." She stepped back from the sink and marched into her bedroom.

.   .   .

Alexander was too exhausted to think about his relationship with Mel, his new mission to spy on the massage parlor, or his report to Inspector Grimble about his visit to Wiremu Wilson's pot-growing operation. He soon fell asleep but was jolted awake when he heard a noise.

He sat upright and imagined Mel had walked into the room, naked. Instead he was greeted with darkness. He quietly rose and peeked out of the window. He had parked the Holden in such a way he could see who would take it in the morning. He still had the keys in his jeans pocket. Wiremu had instructed him to leave the car keys on top of the inside front tire.

No one was on the street.

.   .   .

Mel found him dressed, on the window seat.

"Good morning."

She was aloof, formal, reserved.

Alexander made a sad face.

"Did you sleep okay?" she asked, ignoring his expression.

"No. I'm banished to the sofa, I can't stop thinking about you, and there was a strange noise last night. I couldn't sleep."

"Yes, I heard it too. Thought it was you falling on the floor."

"Funny." Alexander ran his hands through his hair as he looked at her. Despite his infatuation, or was it his obsession with her, he could not decipher her mood. She had not come out to see if he had fallen off the sofa. It would have been a great way to make up. They could have made love on the carpet again like the first time, at least the first time in her house. She was not quite mocking him and not quite annoyed at him, but there was little warmth in her demeanor.

"I've made coffee," she said. "I'm going to shower and dress, then we can talk."

Is she disappointed I didn't try to steal into her bed? Would she have thrown me out? Or snuggled next to me, even if we didn't make love?

She sat across from him on the window seat, her wet hair pulled back. She wore a dark-green trouser suit and Alexander wanted to hold her face in his hands and tenderly kiss her but instead he held the cover of the Small Faces album he had just put on. His Nikon with the telephoto lens was on his knees.

"You never told me about the significance of that Small Faces album. You started to dance to 'I Feel Much Better' and you want me to check out the massage parlor. What's the connection? I feel there is one."

Mel registered no emotion as she undid her hair. She shook out her curls, spraying Alexander with drops of water.

He closed his eyes and allowed himself a small smile before looking at her again. "And it's something you've never told anyone else."

She did not react.

He took a deep breath. "And it's got something to do with, what, over ten years ago? So it's not about your childhood, but when you were a student."

He paused again to see if he was heading in the right direction. "No. A medical student. Something happened when you were in Otago. And it was something really bad. A secret? Too awful to recount, but you still live with it, don't you. Every time you hit a man, it's redemption. So it's sexual. Just like what's happening to those girls, I mean women, at the Flamingo."

Mel had remained impassive throughout his questioning, which Alexander thought was a sign in itself.

"I have to get to work," she said, but remained seated.

"I know you want to tell me. You can trust me with your secret. There's no one else who can listen and care for you like I can. Who's more deeply committed to you? Despite what you think of me." Alexander went to hold her hands. She looked at him and did not break away.

"Can you turn it off?" she asked quietly.

Alexander lifted the needle off the album. He came back to the window seat and sat opposite her. He glanced at the Holden, touched his camera and stared into the gold flecks of her amber eyes. He could not explain what was happening to his insides.

"You're very sweet, but I have to go. We'll talk later. I promise." Mel sprang up with her coffee mug, leaned over to kiss his forehead and ran to the kitchen. "Lock the door when you leave and call me tonight after you've been there," she shouted from the hall.

Alexander watched her BMW disappear, still intoxicated by her kiss despite its chasteness.

He turned his attention to Wiremu's car. Was the noise in the night related to the car? At the front entrance he scanned the street before he walked to the Holden to open the driver's door. Inside he felt under the seats and banged on the door panels. He wondered if there were hidden packages. He sat in the back seat and felt the doors and the roof lining before he got out and opened the trunk. It was big enough for two bodies, he thought. Lifting the old carpet he saw the rusted metal underneath, but no hidden compartment and no spare tire.

He was about to slam the trunk shut when he stepped back and studied the rear of the sedan again and compared the size with the interior of the trunk. He leaned inside and pushed his right hand against where the rear seat should be. There was carpet against some wood, plywood he thought from the sound as he knocked again across what he now suspected was a fake partition. His back ached and he hit his head on the trunk lid. When the stars disappeared, he scanned the road again. No one was in sight. He took photos of the trunk, the car and the number plates, front and back, with his Rollei 35 before he locked the car and left the keys on top of the front tire facing the house.

Back inside, he placed the needle back on the LP and sat by the window, his Nikon focused on the car. He had been outplayed, having transported maybe fifty pounds of marijuana in a hidden compartment to Auckland, and Wiremu would no longer need him to offload a mere five pounds. He had no idea when someone would arrive to take the car. He thought about dismantling the partition and photographing the hidden treasure, but it was too much of a gamble.

Alexander wanted to call Grimble right away. The phone was in the kitchen. If he ran to the kitchen to call Grimble and missed the person who took the car, Grimble would be mad at him for not getting the photos. If he stayed at his post and captured photos of the person who took the car, Grimble would still be mad at him for not calling him right away.

The album was still playing as he wondered how he could get into Mel's mind. He almost missed seeing a young man, dressed all in denim and wearing long dreadlocks, walk around the Holden. Alexander managed to capture the man as he bent down on the driver's side to retrieve the keys. He kept shooting as the man slipped into the car, started it, executed a slow turn and disappeared toward Mount Eden Road.

He leapt from the window seat to call Grimble.

"You what?" Grimble shouted. "You let him get away?"

"I couldn't phone you beforehand. The phone's in the kitchen. What if he turned up while I was calling you and I never got the photos? I've got some good shots of him."

"Describe him."

Alexander closed his eyes and recited what he saw through his viewfinder.

"Did you recognize him?"

"No, never seen him before, but I'm going to the gallery now to develop the photos and I'll bring them right over. I've got Wiremu's entire operation."

"And the number plate? Did you get that?"

Alexander repeated it twice.

"Hurry." Grimble hung up.

.   .   .

He pressed the plastic prong into the clear liquid and watched the image appear on the 8 x 10 sheet. The blacks were deep, and the grays had enough contrast to show the outline of dozens of marijuana plants suspended from ropes in the large barn. He had overexposed the outer edges of the print so he could get more detail from the low light.

The other prints had been easier to develop and told a story of a vast hidden operation. He could not believe how well the photos had come out, considering he had to guess the exposure, the distance, and where to aim his hidden camera.

Alexander walked from the gallery's darkroom to the empty library where he knew he could make a free long-distance call. He hoped to catch Deborah at home in Wellington.

She answered on the first ring. "Kia ora."

"Kei te pehea koe."

"Tell me in te reo."

"You're kidding. I've about exhausted my Maori."

"Then you need extra lessons," Deborah said. "Are you here in Wellington?"

"No. I'm just back in Auckland. Had some adventures up north."

"Are you going to tell me about them?"

"The marae visits went better than expected. I thought I was going to be, I don't know, vilified? But I've gained a new understanding of Maori. Maoritanga. It was magical, before all the dope I was offered."

"Oh, no, Alexander. You didn't get high did you? I thought you were a Blue Nun and Southern Comfort kind of guy."

"I am. I never want to inhale that stuff again."

"Bad things happen to people who do drugs. You didn't bring any back did you?"

"Deborah, you know me better than that."

"I just worry about you. When am I going to see you next? I miss you. You're so much fun. I could give you another lesson. Wouldn't it be cool?"

"Cool? You've never used that word."

"I'm a librarian. I have a wide vocabulary at my disposal. I'm very talented and diverse."

"Oh." Alexander sighed. His mind was detracted from what he had originally planned to say.

"What's wrong?" Deborah asked.

"There's something I have to tell you, and it can't wait till I get back, so I'm going to have to tell you over the phone, and I hope you can forgive me. It seems unfair and cruel but I have to do it, and I know you have something to tell me as well. I don't know what it is exactly, but you weren't entirely honest with me, were you? Over the doctor and my photos."

In the silence, Alexander could hear her heavy breathing through her nose.

"So here's my confession. It's been eating away at me, and it's the only thing I can think of. I just have to come out and say it. It would be better if I said what I have to say in person, but I can't, so here goes." He stopped to take a deep breath.

"You can't keep me in suspense," Deborah said.

"I'm with someone else here in Auckland. I told her about you and she's rejected me. It happened the day I flew here. It seems I can't be with two women. It doesn't work, and it's unfair. To everyone. I've probably ruined the relationship. I have to be honest with you, but please, I never wanted to hurt your feelings or let you down."

"You've broken up with her?"

"We're still speaking, barely. Seems I've botched it. I had to talk to you. We can't go on seeing each other. It's not going to work. I'm sorry I'm being so blunt. What do you say?"

"Well. I knew you were with someone there, just like you were with me here in Wellington." Deborah sighed. "I didn't mind."

She seemed so understanding and compliant, but then Alexander heard her gasp. Could he hear tears of sadness or rage? This confused him. He shook his head and continued.

"You were going to tell me something, weren't you? And I appreciate your honesty, I think. But there is something else?" He could feel her breathing. He imagined her in her apartment, naked but for a robe, with her long red hair flowing down her back. He scanned the library to confirm he was alone. He waited.

Her breathing changed.

"You're right, I should have told you, but I didn't want to lose you. But now I have. Lost you, I mean." She paused. "So it doesn't matter, does it?"

"Go on." He knew what would happen if he saw her again.

"My brother returned from Thailand with a suitcase full of hashish. The idiot. I love him but he can make wrong decisions. He said he had a sister who was important in the government and they should talk to her. They being the police, but somehow an SIS man came into the picture. He knew I lived across from Dr. Winter and knew all about you. He made me an offer. I could work for him, keep him informed of what you were doing and help you with your photos, and in return, they would give my brother a suspended sentence. If I co-operated enough, they would let him go. I had no choice. I've always taken care of my brother. He seems to get into messes all the time, but this was serious. He could have gone to prison for years."

"And I thought it was my irresistible charm and good looks."

"Oh, Alexander, don't sell yourself short. You have everything a girl would want. I had so much fun."

"You did the right thing. In a way I'm glad you didn't tell me. I've one question, really. Maybe two. Did the SIS man wear Old Spice, the old-fashioned cologne?"

"Funny you should mention that, because I think he did. I used to get sneezing fits after he left."

"You saw him? At your place?"

"Yes. I had to burn a lot of incense. Why?"

"Just a hunch I had. And the other question. Was it real to you? Us, I mean."

"Oh god, Alexander. It was too good to be true, wasn't it. Why would a young stud like you be interested in a middle-aged woman like me? Overweight, never married, lives alone."

"You're middle-aged? I thought you were only a few years older than me. And you're not overweight. Voluptuous, yes. And extremely seductive, but it's you who shouldn't sell yourself short. You're very beautiful. Like the Klimt poster of *Danaë*. But more so."

"You're too sweet. But can I see you again when you come back, so we can talk?"

Alexander closed his eyes and wondered if he could resist her erotic radiance if he saw her again. He imagined her robe falling open . . .

He opened his eyes when he heard the security guard come into the library and saw him gesture for Alexander to leave.

"I have to go now. I'm being kicked out of the gallery. I'll call you. When I get back."

"Okay. I look forward to seeing you, Alexander."

He could feel the sadness and loneliness in her voice and he wondered if he could have handled the call any better.

The security guard was staring at him from the door.

"I've got to go, goodbye."

He hung up and stared at the phone for a few seconds before he gathered his photographs and his camera bag.

.   .   .

Sergeant Cadd escorted Alexander into Inspector Grimble's office.

"You let a huge shipment of marijuana out of your sight!" Grimble shouted. "And Wiremu Wilson's in town! What are you doing? Who do you work for?"

"Can I sit down and explain? Show you the photos? It was Permanent Under-Secretary Catelin who ordered me to find out about Wiremu Wilson's operation and co-ordinate with you."

Grimble pointed to a chair opposite his desk. Alexander sat next to Cadd and opened the large brown envelope he carried. He spread out the 8 x 10 black-and-white photos of the inside of Wiremu Wilson's marijuana curing and packaging operation. The two policemen were silent as they pored over the photos.

Grimble spread his hands out. "All from your hidden camera?" Grimble asked, keeping a neutral expression. "And why would he show you everything?"

"I left my camera bag and Nikon at their house. I have a new compact point and shoot. I've got it in my denim jacket. Here. It's a Rollei 35."

He stood and with his left hand in his side pocket, pressed the shutter release as he coughed, placing his right hand over his mouth. "It's as small as a packet of cigarettes. All I have to do is set the exposure beforehand and the dis-tance and the wide aperture takes care of the rest. As you can see. It's an amazing lens. And it's a full 35 millimeter negative." Alexander smiled, for now he had captured a candid portrait of Inspector Grimble at his desk.

Cadd bent to see the hole in the side of Alexander's jacket.

"If I turn like so, you can't see the hole. And you wouldn't know it's there."

"Did they search you? Pat you down?" Cadd asked.

"It wasn't that kind of meeting. And they saw I left my camera bag at their place. Besides, I'm a buyer, not a cop."

"Why would they trust you?" Cadd pressed.

"I'm organizing a tour of Maori art. I didn't think Wiremu would be so trusting, so quickly. He can be pretty intimidating, together with his brother, Rawiri."

The sergeant continued to look at the prints.

"Yes. Rawiri and Wiremu. Can't mistake them, even with short hair and clean shaven."

Cadd scrutinized Alexander. "Seems a lot of cannabis. Did you see anything else?" He sorted through a number of ordnance survey maps on top of a large filing cabinet. He selected a map of Hokianga Harbor and unrolled it over the photos. "Can you pinpoint where you were?"

"Yes. But . . ." Alexander shrugged.

Grimble and Cadd hunched over the topographic map. "Well, what?" Grimble asked.

"They put a blindfold on me when they left their house. Here's the house." He leaned over the desk and pointed to a turn in the road on the south side of the harbor.

Cadd squinted as he read the map. "Motukiore Road, sir." He turned to Alexander. "And you went north or south?"

"We turned left, so it was south or west. There were a few turns, then it sounded like gravel, then dirt. I could feel the tires on the old Holden bouncing over ruts. We climbed for some time, and I couldn't see any sign of a track when they took the blindfold off. Just trees and the huge barn, hidden between other tall trees."

"How big was their organization?" Grimble asked.

"I was in one large barn. And there were these huge speakers. They were playing Jimi Hendrix and Janis Joplin when I was there. Loud Sixties rock. Real loud."

Cadd moved his finger along the road as he followed Alexander's description until he came to an area marked with tracks. He looked at Grimble, who frowned.

"Can't you raid the place now based on these photos?" Alexander offered.

"I don't think anyone is keen on busting those guys on their own land, no matter how much cannabis they're growing." Grimble scratched his chin.

"You're the cops." Alexander shrugged and sat back in his chair.

Cadd and Grimble exchanged glances.

"He thinks I can deal some of his weed," Alexander said. "I've already got an order for five pounds of the stuff. Cash on delivery and he thinks I can take another five. All the artists and their dealers I know want large quantities. There's a drought on and demand is high."

Cadd let out a whistle.

"He told me he'd call me at Mel's place in a few days. I thought it would be a good time for you to move in or at least know when he was coming to Auckland."

Grimble knotted his eyebrows. "Did someone ask you to set up a buy?"

"No, not in so many words, but I was given explicit instructions by Catelin to get inside his organization, and I made a strategic decision on the spot. What else could I have said to win his confidence? Then he offered me his car to get back to Auckland."

Alexander took another envelope out of his inside denim pocket.

They stared at a large, dark young man dressed in military clothing reaching for the keys on the front tire, making a four-point turn, then driving away in a blur to Mount Eden Road. Long hair obscured the man's face.

Grimble grimaced. "So he played you. He had no intention of selling you five pounds. He used you for this shipment."

"Maybe. But we don't know yet, do we? And he doesn't know I know I brought down a shipment for him, and documented it. What I'm doing is helping you build a complete case. Correct? One small arrest with a bit player isn't going to destroy Wiremu's entire network, is it?"

He looked for support at Cadd, who turned to Grimble. Alexander noticed for the first time a large whiteboard behind him with names and photographs of people. "And I take it you don't know who he is?"

Cadd gave a small shrug.

"You have to call me as soon as Wiremu calls you," Grimble ordered. "If he does call you. Get as much detail as possible about any rendezvous he's going to arrange. He'll likely use someone else you won't know. We'll plan everything we can, but I want to keep you as uninvolved as possible. You understand? No spy antics."

Alexander raised his hands. "Drugs scare me. I don't want to have anything to do with the shipment."

"You've no idea how many young men have told me the same thing, and went to prison."

Grimble ushered Alexander and Cadd to the elevators.

"When Wiremu or whoever contacts you, call me immediately. Any time. They'll put you through."

Alexander read out the number on the back of the inspector's business card and asked if they had found Wiremu's Holden.

Grimble held out his hand and Alexander felt the strong fingers almost crush his as their eyes locked.

CHAPTER EIGHTEEN

Alexander had backed the car into an empty parking lot. He switched off the lights of his rental, a 1970 Datsun 510 two-door, and moved to the rear seat, his Nikon with the telephoto lens aimed at the Flamingo's entrance. Grimble had recommended the company he had rented the car from, in Eden Terrace. The sedan smelt of cigarette smoke and was as dirty inside as it was on the outside. He thought it was perfect for his new surveillance job, with no streetlights nearby, invisible. The color of the car was a mystery to him—the manager of the car lot said it was burnt orange, and Alexander thought it was a 410 from 1965, but the price was right.

He kept watch on the car park opposite. A couple of older men staggered through the front door and disappeared. A large neon sign on the roof provided the only illumination. It was after midnight. Other cars were parked nearby but the street was deserted.

A new Jaguar XJ6 pulled up to the front door. A solidly built man in a blazer stepped out and scanned his surroundings. He stopped to stare at the Datsun parked opposite before striding into the parlor as if he owned the place.

Alexander had managed one shot of the staring man then counted to a hundred before he crossed the street. He stepped into the foyer and came to the counter, a glass table with bare wooden boards wrapped around it. The walls were lined with oiled pine planks. Two women behind the counter watched him. They wore white towels, barely concealing their thin bodies. A red lightbulb hung from the ceiling and Alexander could just read the price list thrust at him. He opted for a sauna, a towel and a back massage followed by a bubble bath. He counted out twenty-dollar bills from his roll. The girls' unsmiling eyes watched him.

"Tipping is extra and if you need any additional services you have to talk to the girl," the younger woman with garish eye make-up said. "We're very strict here."

Alexander was given a locker key on a rubber band, which he put on his wrist, and was shown to the dressing room. He folded his clothes and placed them on top of his shoes in a rusty locker. He had cash and his car keys hidden in one shoe but was unsure how secure the lock was. Wrapped in a towel, he wandered barefoot through narrow corridors of pine planks until he came to the sauna. He pushed a heavy wooden door open and stepped into the dark space. A large bald man with a hairy body rose from a corner and hobbled out.

Alexander could smell onions and beer in the empty sauna. He was in a world far away from his art gallery and he wondered what he was doing here until he remembered he had to win Mel back, at whatever cost. An electric sauna unit was in one corner with dry stones on top of the glowing red elements. A bucket of water with a wooden paddle was beside the unit. He poured some water over the stones, expecting to cool them. Instead, he was assaulted with thick clouds of steam. He could not breathe, it was so hot and humid, way beyond his Wellington-based senses. He saw a speaker in the corner and heard a crackling sound. It could have been music, but he was unsure of the tune.

He heard his name called, over the intercom, to room eight. Sweat dripped from his forehead and he felt dizzy as he staggered out and made two attempts wandering through the corridors until he found a narrow pine door marked "8". He opened the door and could make out a young girl with scruffy hair and a white towel wrapped around her tiny body. She was barefoot. Alexander could see the room had just enough space for a massage table, a brown vinyl slab about six feet long and two feet wide. A small red bulb hung from the low ceiling.

She pointed to the table. "On your stomach, and you can take off your towel if you're comfortable."

"Fine. My name's—" His mind went blank. He was about to be naked in front of a stranger and he had forgotten his name. "Doug. What's yours?"

"Tiffany."

Alexander eased himself onto the table and looked back at her. The vinyl felt sticky: there was no sheet or towel between his body and the thin table. He should have lain on the small towel but it was on the floor now, and he had no desire to retrieve it.

Tiffany poured oil directly onto his back. It felt cold and he could not identify the smell.

"Is this okay?" she asked.

"Fine."

She had a light touch and worked her hands along his spine. Not a trained masseuse, he thought as he tried to relax, feeling like a turkey about to be basted as the surplus oil dripped onto the sides of the table.

·   ·   ·

Mel marched him to the bathroom when she opened the front door. She had been reading Rosemary McLeod's *A Girl Like I* in bed, and had her long red satin robe wrapped tight around her.

"When you come out, you can tell me what happened," she stated, all business.

After a long hot shower, Alexander appeared in the hallway, dressed in his remaining clean white shirt and jeans. He made a note to himself to get his blue suit and shirts dry-cleaned. He breathed in. "I still stink of the oil. It's disgusting. Can you make me a cup of tea, please?"

"Nothing stronger?"

"No. I need my wits about me to recall everything I saw."

"Well, I'm listening."

Alexander followed her to the kitchen.

"I thought I was the last one there. Had a mediocre massage, went to another room for a bubble bath and the young woman who attended me was so skinny, she looked like she hadn't eaten in a week."

"What was her name?"

"Tiffany. She'd be cute with her clothes on. She looks so young and innocent, and lost."

"Your type?"

"Oh, no. *You're* my type."

"How come?"

"Strong, assertive, and you know what you want. And you have—" Alexander stopped himself with a smile.

"Go on."

"Ugh! I felt so unclean there. It was unpleasant. The only halfway decent part was the sauna. It was hot, too hot for me. And there was a lingering aroma there I found nasty.

So halfway through my bubble bath, I heard a loud noise outside, footsteps and shouting. My girl, Tiffany, panicked. I mean, her eyes bulged and she started trembling. I asked what was the matter. And, well, you have to picture me. I was naked in a shallow round bathtub with very few bubbles, and she had a sponge. I swear it was not new, or clean.

"And she just freezes. I ask her again what's the matter and she shakes her head. 'Don't ask,' she whispers, drops the sponge and runs out. I never see her again.

"I did hear some shouting and thuds, I think. I waited a few minutes then got out of the tub, went back to the locker and got dressed. At the front counter, I returned my key and complained to the girl there. The other one with too much eye make-up had gone."

"You said her name was Tiffany?"

"Yes."

"Small, blond, timid-looking, longish hair?"

"Yes. You know her? She's a patient?"

"They didn't offer you a refund or anything?"

"Ah. She *is* a patient."

"I can't tell you that, Alexander."

"I asked what happened to my girl and she just shrugged. I pulled out a couple of twenties and left them for Tiffany. I don't know if they'll give her the money but at least I made an impression. I think."

"Do you feel comfortable going back?"

"Yes, why not? I might go earlier, say, before the pubs close. I'm sure they get a lot of drunks coming there." Alexander finished his tea and burped. "And there's something else I found interesting."

Mel kept staring at him.

"You sent me there. Don't get jealous, and don't expect me to find out a lot the first time. They'll think I'm a cop if I ask questions."

"You're almost a cop. You're a spy."

"Different. But I'll take it as a compliment. Now I think about it, it *is* strange."

"What? You can't keep me hanging."

"There was a large mirror in the bubble-bath room. It didn't mist up and she kept staring at it, but not at her reflection. It felt weird."

"Maybe she was checking you out?"

"No. She was so cold, so was the water. I think she thought someone was behind the mirror looking at her, maybe with a camera? I don't know. I'll have to check out the space next time I'm there. It's probably hidden because I couldn't see any room next to it. It's what I would do. There's got to be a secret door."

"Did you sign in? And give an address?"

"Don't worry. I did as we agreed. I used a phony Wellington address and I was Doug McLeish. Although sometimes I put the i before the e."

"The trade union leader? He's always in the news."

"I could be his young cousin."

"Sounds risky."

"Doubt it." Alexander smiled with exaggerated calm. He could not tell if she was leading him on, or if he was sleeping on the sofa. The sofa was better than being thrown out of her house. In the silence, he asked: "Tiffany. One of your patients. Maybe if I see her again she might be less guarded?"

"We'll have to see. Anyway, what really happened in Northland? Are you getting your exhibition?"

"Yes. It's all taken care of. Went really well. Took lots of photos and I saw, in fact I hung out with your friend Wiremu and his half-brother, Rawiri. Although I already knew of them."

"Wiremu. Does he still have short hair and look respectable?"

"I don't know about looking respectable but he has short hair. Supposed to be the biggest pot grower in Hokianga. I can't even begin to describe what they have. It's beyond my experience. And it seems I am somehow related to them because of a Russian bear. It's a long and weird story. I'll fill you in when we're both not so tired."

"A bear? How much did you smoke?"

"Too much, it seems. Just to let them know I was okay with it. I'll never do it again. Made me paranoid. Then I passed out on the floor of their house. Really weird. I'll stick to wine, thank you."

"Take any photos?"

"Oh, I tried to, but was careful. I don't think they trust me."

"What do you mean?"

"Well, the next morning, they blindfolded me then took me on a tour of a forest, a really secluded place. Saw their stored pot, their curing barn, a couple of trucks hidden away. It's a big operation and a little scary."

"Scary?"

"Well, you know Wiremu."

"Yes. I think I do."

"And the car was picked up by somebody I don't know, so it's no longer outside."

"Yes, I noticed. I'm going to bed now. You can sleep on the sofa." She turned and headed to her bedroom. Alexander stood there, helpless.

He arranged some blankets and stared at the sound system. There was only a faint light from a streetlight creeping into the room. The curtain was not fully drawn and the window was open but no cool air came inside. It was as hot inside as outside. He was wondering if he could get a large photo he had taken of Hokianga Harbor framed and placed on the wall when he heard a noise.

Mel walked in, wrapped in her red robe, her hair tied back and a determined look in her eyes. She sat in a chair opposite Alexander and placed her face in her hands. "I can't sleep," she said. "It's too humid."

"Nor can I." He was dying to walk over and hold her, in his T-shirt and boxers. Instead he recounted the story Wiremu told him. "It's a very Russian story. Bringing two Russian bears halfway around the world, brother and sister, to start a new colony of bears in New Zealand. Then to go fishing in the sea and not know how to swim and drown."

Mel kept her eyes on him. "You never talk about your parents, do you?" she said. "What happened to your father?"

Alexander told her about his father, Arkadi Davidovich Newton. "It's just a recollection of stories," he concluded. "When I retell them they seem made up, embellished, like fairy tales. Russian fairy tales." He shrugged and stared at the carpet, occasionally glancing at her legs, the way she hugged herself, the way her hair had slipped over her shoulders.

"You don't want to find your mother?" she asked.

"My mother abandoned us early on. I have no idea how old I was. Nothing good would come of finding her. If she's dead, I would mourn her. But alive? We wouldn't reconcile. There are too many questions and, I suppose, recriminations I have for her. Why she abandoned me, my father. It's better I don't know. I don't want to face the consequences. Unintended though they may be. Yes, unintended consequences. I don't want them. Look at me now. The mess I'm in with you. I've never felt like I've felt being with you, even if we are apart now. At least I am still in your house. Right? Be with you, sort of."

Alexander raised his eyes to see her holding her knees. His mind racing with all the possibilities. He shuddered and returned his gaze to the carpet.

"Don't you think it's Freudian? Denying your mother. I'm sure you could find her."

"No. It's got nothing to do with Freud. And I'm not fixated on older women, either."

He had a flash of Deborah, how she had described herself as middle-aged and overweight. He had never seen Deborah in daylight, never met her for lunch or taken her out to dinner. All their encounters had taken place in her dimly lit bedroom. And now he wanted to get into Mel's bedroom. Mel, he calculated, was probably ten years older than him, but he did not want to raise that as he copied Mel's body language, drew his legs in and hugged his knees. He checked he was not showing anything in his boxers.

"Talking of fixing things, I called her today and broke up with her. The Maori teacher."

"She's Maori?"

"Partly, and she's a librarian. She confessed to how she was blackmailed by the security services to spy on me. Something to do with her brother caught importing drugs from Thailand. If she worked for them, her brother would go free. So I feel quite used. It's over. Finished. Now I haven't a girlfriend in Wellington and it appears I don't have a girlfriend in Auckland." Alexander pushed his long hair back from his face and waited for a response.

"We'll see. Now I really have to go to sleep. I'll talk to you in the morning."

She left the room without turning back.

Before Alexander fell asleep, he imagined he was standing with Mel on the summit of Mount Eden. The sun rose above Rangitoto. The sky changed colors as the sounds of the city awakening rose to them. He breathed in her fragrance, her hair, her smile, and her amber eyes changing as light came into the world.

CHAPTER NINETEEN

Beverly Jarvis waltzed into the hallway, checked her face at the starburst mirror and pushed back her long blond hair. She threw her car keys into a pottery bowl on the kitchen counter and turned to her husband in the dark, watching television in his favorite chair in the living room. They occupied a ranch house at the end of a cul-de-sac in Takapuna.

"Are you watching your favorite series? What is it? Ngaio Marsh? They always catch the killer, don't they, darling?" She heard a grunt and switched on the kitchen light that bled over to where he sat. "Not like real life is it?" she added, and waited for a response.

When none came she poked her head into the living room. "Did you get your dinner from the fridge?" She turned and saw he had left the plate next to the sink, with the lamb bones and congealed gravy.

"Where were you?" he asked. He had an empty beer bottle in his hand.

"Out with Babs, my old school friend? We had game night with the girls." She adjusted her hair again and her cheeks appeared flushed.

Jarvis eased himself out of his chair and rose to his full height. "That car. I've been meaning to talk to you about it." He walked into the kitchen to put the bottle by the sink and fixed his blue eyes on his wife. Even in sweatpants and a T-shirt he looked distinguished with his perfect short white hair and strong jaw.

Beverly looked at the bottle. He never cleaned up after himself. She thought she would save her argument for another time.

"I got a great deal from Barbara. And I have my own money, remember? I've paid for it. It's all above board. You don't have to worry about anything. I'd never do anything to cause you embarrassment, darling." She went to kiss him on his check.

"Is that tequila on your breath?" he asked as he wiped the lipstick from his face.

"Just had one, dear."

He put his hands on his hips. "Beverly Jarvis, I've told you about that before."

"Superintendent, you're in charge. No one is going to ticket me for drunk driving. Besides, I wouldn't want to damage my car."

"That's the point." Jarvis's blue eyes became wider as he registered what she was wearing: red hot pants, white go-go boots and a red shirt tied at the midriff showing her tanned stomach. "And aren't those from the Sixties? I mean, how long have you had them?" he asked, raising his eyebrows and voice. "Were you out in public in that?"

"Don't be silly, darling. We all dress up for our girls' night. It's part of the fun." She made *darling* sound like she meant *shithead*, but in a nice way.

She left him with his mouth open as she waltzed into her bedroom and shut the door.

CHAPTER TWENTY

"**D**o you know anything about Sergeant Bradshaw?"

"Yes, sir. Went to the Police College with him."

"Tell me about him."

"I don't like speaking ill of anyone on the Force, sir."

"Come on, Sergeant Cadd. It's me asking. Spit it out."

"At Trentham he always took the easy way out, sucked up to his teachers, sold anyone out for his own good. Not loyal, or trustworthy, or anything good."

"So you don't like him?" Grimble glanced at Cadd while he drove the Falcon.

Cadd kept his eyes on the Southern Motorway and avoided his boss's eyes.

"I wasn't impressed. Don't know how he made sergeant. Remember how we talked about being a good smart copper, and not changing the rules to suit the arrest?"

"Yes."

"Well, I think he can be bought."

"You mean he's corrupt?"

"I have no proof, but I get the feeling he's on the take. Check out his car while we're there."

They were silent as Inspector Grimble drove toward Pukekohe.

"You look fit, Cadd. Running again?"

"Yes, sir. When I can. Back to my old waist size." Cadd patted his flat stomach. "No beer gut. I stopped drinking. When you reach a certain age it just sticks to your belly."

Grimble glanced at his own waist.

"I've been running longer and longer and now head out to Epsom. I've even run past Barbara Turner's place a few times."

"But it's a dead-end street. Did you see her?"

"Actually, I got to see her twice. If you're dressed the part, early in the morning you can run anywhere. She was in her housecoat, watering the garden with a hose, or sitting on her patio, smoking."

"Did she see you?"

"Don't think so."

"Don't be so sure. She doesn't miss a trick."

Grimble took the Drury turn to Pukekohe.

.   .   .

Cadd scanned Manukau Road, the single-story shops, the red brick buildings with tin roofs and overhangs. "Like going back in time here."

"I liked the Fifties."

Grimble parked adjacent to the police station, next to a patrol car on the pavement. He spotted a bright yellow, brand-new 1976 Holden utility parked on the street, and looked at Cadd, who nodded.

They walked into a converted house. Grimble showed his ID to the constable at the front desk. Sergeant Bradshaw appeared and offered to take them to a coffee shop called Oldham's on King Street nearby.

Bradshaw was just as Grimble expected him to be. A former rugby player who had expanded in the middle, and eyes that could bore through you. Bradshaw acknowledged his old classmate Cadd with a nod.

They walked to the café and sat at a table with their coffees.

Grimble addressed Bradshaw. "Sergeant Bradshaw, tell us about the Looks. I understand you've had some dealings with them."

"Call me Will, sir. All my friends do." Bradshaw smiled and showed his teeth.

"Sergeant Bradshaw, when did you last see the Looks?"

"About two weeks ago, sir. I was aware they might be growing something other than tomatoes in those greenhouses of theirs, so I paid them a friendly visit. You can never keep track of their extended family. Always travelling. And their family patriarch, Sam Look, you can't get anything out of him other than it's going to rain sometime soon. You've seen my report?"

Grimble glanced at Cadd then continued. "Did you inspect the greenhouses?"

"Wouldn't I need a search warrant, sir? I like to do everything by the book. As we were taught, eh, Sergeant Cadd?"

"But you could always ask for advice on growing tomatoes. Ask to see the greenhouses. Make some pretense?" Grimble raised his eyebrows. "The community policeman? Friendly-like?"

"Yes, sir. I realize that, but they were downright hostile and didn't offer any information. I tried, but they wouldn't let me into their house, that's Bruce Look's house. Spent all my time at the front door." Bradshaw kept his head lowered.

The inspector turned to his sergeant. He knew Cadd could read his reaction. "You wouldn't mind if we paid them a visit, would you?" he asked with forced politeness.

"Not at all, inspector. Anything I can do to help, just ask me, sir. I am at your service."

· · ·

When Grimble turned off the main road and headed toward the Look's property, he said, "What did you think of your old mate?"

"Well, he's put on some weight. And I don't buy him standing at the front door and not barging his way in or walking around to the greenhouses to see for himself."

"What else?"

"*By the book*?" Cadd shook his head in disbelief. "In his defense, you'd want him by your side in a bar fight or street brawl. He has his moments."

"Generous of you, Cadd. Remind me to run a check on him and his new car when we get back."

· · ·

There were no cars parked outside the Looks' house. Cadd pounded on the door several times and rang the doorbell repeatedly.

"Shall we?" he asked.

They walked to the back and tried knocking on the kitchen door, then they walked around the property, over a small rise, until they saw the four greenhouses in a small valley. Before them lay rows and rows of lettuces and other vegetables. They called out but heard no reply then walked down the track to the greenhouses. When they came to the fourth, Grimble opened the glass door and stepped inside. There was a faint whiff, raw and herbal in nature.

"Smells like weed, sir. But there's nothing here, is there. Funny, the other three have mature tomato plants. Beefsteak, I think. But why is this one empty?" Cadd knelt and ran his hands over the earth. He scooped up dirt to sift through his fingers. "Nothing."

"And why isn't anyone here, do you think?"

"Because he called them and warned them we were coming."

"Christ almighty! I shouldn't have told him what we were going to do. My mistake, sergeant."

"Not necessarily, sir. We know two things so far."

"And they are?"

"He did call them. Which means he *is* in their pay, as we suspected. And they were growing pot here, but it's cleaned out. And look." Cadd bent down further into the greenhouse, and ran his hands over the soft dry earth again. "There are a few leaves and sticks here. We could take samples. Come back with a search warrant."

"That's more than two things. But they couldn't have got rid of it all in what, half an hour?"

"Which leads us to the next question, sir. Where did they put everything? Which leads to another question. If they have harvested the entire crop, where is it?"

"Maybe it's a new type of cannabis. Don't think we have enough for a search warrant here. Not yet. But I want to work on Bradshaw. If he is in this, we need to include him. Let's go back."

Grimble surveyed the property and saw another ridge and the top of a large pine tree. Cadd followed him back to the driveway. He squinted for an instant as he looked back into the valley.

"What now?" Grimble said as they walked to the car. "We can't use what we've seen here as we didn't have access. We can't use what Sergeant Bradshaw has seen or not seen as we can't trust him. So we start with the weakest link. Him. The Looks aren't going to tell us anything. Are we going to stake out their place for a month to see what happens?"

"Yes sir, I understand."

Inside the Ford, Cadd's face brightened. "We could take your car to the Pukekohe Raceway now. They'd let us burn some rubber. Don't you want to see what it can do?"

"Cadd, please. I don't want to give Jarvis any ammunition and have him take the car away from me. I think he's already mad I got the car. Don't know why he's so fixated on it. He usually doesn't care or notice. And it would be a perfect excuse. You understand this doesn't go further, Cadd?"

"Yes sir. It never does."

"Down here, it's a small town. Everyone knows everyone else's business. Let's get back."

CHAPTER TWENTY-ONE

"Can we not talk about Wiremu? More coffee?"

They were in her kitchen. Mel was showered and dressed for work. Alexander was in his rumpled T-shirt and jeans. She refilled his mug. It could have been an idyllic domestic scene, he thought, but he had spent a sleepless night on the sofa thinking about her and how desperately he wanted to be with her, in every way.

"Do you keep in touch with your parents?" Alexander had wanted to ask her for ages—he had been struggling to become aware of other people and how they viewed the world and their relationships, what connections they had, what they thought of each other. He had no personal references on how to relate to parents.

"Yes. In fact, I was supposed to see them on Sunday afternoon." She smiled. They were listening to a jazz record Alexander had found, *Song for My Father* by Horace Silver.

"And what does your father do?"

"He's a GP. In St Heliers. Near where they live."

"So you followed in his footsteps. He must be proud."

"No. Disappointed."

She suddenly looked very serious. "What about your parents and your kung fu classes?"

"They disapprove. Then there was the trial, the family name in the papers."

"Trial?"

"I was a witness. One of my students defended herself when she was attacked by her boyfriend. Police charged her with manslaughter. I testified as to how I taught her and all the women in my class for self-defense. I don't teach any attack moves. She used a technique I taught, and they tried to blame me for teaching a woman how to defend herself against a larger, aggressive male."

"What happened?"

"The jury acquitted her. The judge was angry, the police were unhappy. The papers were outraged. What if all women fought back? It unnerves a lot of males."

"Is that why Inspector Grimble is so circumspect around you?"

"Could be. Are you going to the Flamingo tonight?"

"Oh, it's the Flamingo now? I need to do some surveillance first."

Alexander stood and ran his hands through his hair. He wanted to approach Mel but she repelled him with her eyes. "I'll knock when I get back. You'll let me in, right?'

"Get out."

.   .   .

As part of his plan for a second trip to the massage parlor, Alexander returned the Datsun to Grimble's contact in Eden Terrace and changed to a Hillman Avenger with an indescribable color. Was it tan or yellow or stale mustard? As a curator he should have been able to identify it.

He was annoyed about everything: how Mel had treated him, the color of his rental car, the tasteless takeaway food he had eaten in Newmarket, and now the endless wait in an obscure parking lot. He hoped the owner of the parlor would not notice his car parked further away, but with a clear view of the entrance.

He backed into the space, turned off his lights and, in the dark, eased his seat back. In his notebook he wrote down who went in and out and at what times. He had his telephoto lens handy but rationed taking photos because of the poor light. His plan was to spend a couple of hours hidden then drive around the block, hide his camera and park again. Eventually he spotted a tall, skinny man get out of an older Mercedes-Benz the size of a Panzer tank, and walk into the parlor. Later a dark-colored Jaguar pulled up and a man dressed in a blazer and khaki pants strode into the parlor. Alexander took photos of both men and decided to follow the man in the blazer after waiting a suitable time.

Doug McLeish signed in at the desk. The woman in a white towel and garish make-up told him the specials and took his money. He ordered the same as the night before. She acted as if she had never seen him before. He took his towel and locker key to the changing room. The man in the blazer was nowhere to be seen and Alexander calculated he could not have signed in and changed in the time it took him to arrive at his locker. He saw three men sitting together in the sauna, a little awkward with their towels stretched around enlarged bellies. A tall, skinny man with a bald spot sat on the top plank. Alexander recognized all four from his surveillance.

He shut the door and walked further along the corridor to where he had his massage. At the next corner he came to what he thought looked like a hidden door. Even with poor lighting he could see there were gaps in the vertical pine slats, but no handle or door hinges. He was about to press on what he thought was the door when it started to move outwards. He saw loafers and khaki pants before he turned around quickly. When he got to the next corner he moved his head slightly and caught a glimpse of the man in a blazer going the other way. Probably back to the counter, Alexander thought.

He found a place in the sauna on the top plank, along from the tall, balding man, rearranged his towel and stretched out. No one talked. The tall man kept looking at him so Alexander smiled back. "Hot, isn't it?" he said.

"Right, mate. Would have to be I reckon. It's a sauna." They laughed. "Lance Beefeater. From Hamilton. Pleased to meet you." He stuck out his hand and Alexander leaned over and shook it. A firm, wet handshake.

"Doug McLeish. From Wellington. You came from Hamilton?"

"Yeah, mate. Suicide city to the wicked big city. Get my kicks." Lance winked at Doug from Wellington. "Know what I mean?"

"Oh yes, Lance. Kinda getting the feel of the place. Last time I missed out on the ending of my bubble bath. Hope to get it this time."

"Yeah. Know what that's like. Bit expensive but cheaper than a date. Right?"

"Oh yeah." Doug from Wellington wiped his forehead and sweat flew everywhere.

Lance sighed. "But a root's a root."

Alexander did not know how to respond, so he leaned back and allowed sweat to run into his eyes, before he heard Lance's name called on the intercom for room nine. Lance climbed down as he adjusted his towel around his narrow waist.

"Good luck, mate." Alexander called out. Lance waved back at Doug from Wellington, as he turned a corner. The sauna door took forever to close.

Alexander was called to room eight. He was greeted by the same blond masseuse, all bones and legs, with a thin towel covering her torso and a faint smile on her face.

"My name is Tiffany. I have you for a full massage and bubble bath and extras?"

"Yes, Tiffany. Call me Doug." And Doug from Wellington slid onto the brown vinyl of the massage table, on his stomach with his towel around his buttocks. He felt her pouring cold oil directly onto his back before she started to lightly rub her hands up his spine. Oil ran down his torso and into his towel. She pressed her fingers into his shoulders and then ran her palms across his back. He did not feel confident in her massaging abilities, nor could he relax as he heard the voice of Lance Beefeater in the next room: "Hot diggity! You know how to please a man. Oh, yeah."

.   .   .

Mel opened her front door to a tired, disheveled Alexander.

"You don't look good. Caught something?"

"I hope not. Although I almost got caught snooping around."

"I'll fix a cup of tea and you can tell me all about it. But first you need a shower."

"Do you have carbolic soap? Really strong stuff?"

.   .   .

Alexander stretched out on the kitchen chair and placed his empty teacup back on its saucer. He inspected his nails. He felt clean again.

"There's something, actually a few things, going on there. First, all the girls, I mean women, are scared of the owner. His name, I found out, is Michael. Michael Donnelly. He has a video camera next to room number nine where he records men getting stuff done to them. I met an odd joker, Lance Beefeater, and I'm sure he's starring in Michael's latest production. Has to be blackmail." Alexander rubbed his hands. "Such a great little business venture."

Mel poured him more tea. "I don't know if you approve, or what?"

"Well, in order to understand a bad guy, you have to think like one."

"What about the women?"

"I got the same girl, Tiffany, who was a little nervous, to say the least. And she was hopeless as a masseuse. I could sense her fear, same with the girl at the front desk. He's spooked them."

"Spooked?"

"Yeah. They're afraid of him. He must have done something physical to them. Right?"

"It's why I sent you there. Remember? I'm the doctor."

"Yes, I know. It's just no one's going to tell me anything." He took a sip of tea and glanced warily at Mel. "I've been thinking, maybe I can follow Tiffany home at close of business. Find out where she lives, then work out a way to bump into her, like at a coffee bar or somewhere safe for her, win her confidence and get her to talk. They aren't going to talk there—it's like the walls have ears. What do you think?"

"Yes. You need to talk to at least one of them out of there and away from him. Why not tomorrow? I'll be at the dojo."

"Good idea."

"You still haven't told me what happened."

"Oh, it's nothing. Well, you know how I like to take chances. Calculated opportunities, really."

"No, I don't."

"I had just finished my massage. I decided against the bubble bath—the sponge was disgusting last time. So I walked out and went back to the sauna, only I got lost and found the hidden door again, next to room nine. I was trying to open it when it sprang open and the owner appeared, right in my face. I acted like I was drunk and slurred my words and wobbled backwards, almost falling over and he grabbed me by my right arm and pulled me toward him. He's small but strong."

He rolled up the sleeve of his shirt and showed the fresh bruises.

Mel stood, held his arm and examined him. She grunted before releasing him.

"He drew me close to him and probably could tell from my breath I hadn't been drinking. I just acted frightened. He didn't say anything. He just stared at me for some time without blinking, like he could cut my head off. Then he turned me around and told me to leave. No wonder the girls are afraid of him."

Mel sat, her eyes downcast. "Don't think it's a good idea to go back again."

"I agree. But I later remembered I saw the glow of a video camera just for a second, the back of a screen. He had some set-up there in the tiny space facing the two-way mirror."

"He sounds dangerous."

"Yeah, but so are you. Anyway, how are you? You seem distracted. Not your normal self."

"Thanks for noticing. I get like this now and then."

"I think I know you, and then I realize I don't. You're a mystery."

Mel looked up, gave a little smile then lowered her head again.

"Do you feel melancholy? Listening to too much Leonard Cohen? Or is it me and our relationship, for what it's worth?"

"There you go. First you're serious, then you're joking. It's hard to tell with you."

"Well, humor is like armor, especially when it comes to love." Alexander emptied his teacup and burped. "Do you have any cake?"

Mel went over to the pantry and took out a tin.

"Why do you care about these women?"

"Some are my patients. Between you and me. And besides, they don't have a choice." Mel cut off and handed him a slice of fruitcake on a plate.

"In what they do?"

"Yes. Free will to them is a myth. This is the only thing they think they can do, for the money."

"You're saying they don't have options?"

"Yes."

"Which leads me to the big question. Why do you do kung fu stuff? And why teach?" Alexander smacked his lips and finished the cake. He used his fingers to pick at the crumbs.

Mel toyed with her saucer. "Helped me get through med school."

"There's more to it, isn't there?" Alexander stared at the cake tin.

Mel ignored him. After a long pause she shook her curls away from her face again and looked into his eyes. "Alexander."

"You're an enigma to me," he said. "A mystery. But my instinct tells me there's something you're holding back. Something really important." He sat very still. "Yes, something you've never told anyone before."

She moved a few facial muscles for an instant.

"Yes, it *is* true. You *are* hiding something. Something big. You almost told me earlier, didn't you?"

"Alexander, how can you? That's not fair."

"I do sort of know you." Alexander was half-expecting a punch, a jab, a slap in reply. He was trying to be lighthearted to counter her darker mood.

Mel adjusted her hair again and examined her cup and saucer as if they might tell her what to do. She let out another deep sigh.

"And you never told me why you call yourself Mel instead of Melodie, with an 'ie'. What happened?" He saw a flash of pain cross her face. Then he waited.

She scrutinized him. "Oh, well." She breathed out. "I might as well tell you. I've never told anyone. So excuse me if I stop and start. Okay?"

Alexander stood then sat again, realizing he would not be allowed to hug her.

"Our senior lecturer at Otago Medical School had a reputation for being a ladies' man and like most rumors I didn't think much of it. Besides, back then such a reputation was almost respectable. In my second year I got to know him quite well, I thought, and he invited me back to his house. He always pronounced 'Melodie' in a certain way, it sounds creepy now, but then, I was, I don't know, different. He said he was having a party for some select students who were doing outstanding work.

"When I arrived there were only three other women students, one from my year and two from the first-year class. Didn't think anything of this at the time. Anyway there was nothing to eat and he had us drinking vodka, first Screwdrivers then we progressed to shots. Lots of toasts. I'd never seen him so excited as he was usually reserved, although friendly, but polite to the women students. I went to the bathroom to splash some water on my face and when I returned I found myself alone with him in the kitchen. The others had left together. He became very forward. I asked where his wife was and he ignored me. He held me by my arms and kissed me. And I froze. I didn't know what to do."

Mel took another breath. Her hands were clasped tightly.

"He began to undress me. I wore a dress with a zip in the back. It was summer and back then my hair was all the way to my waist if I didn't put it in a ponytail. He slipped the dress off my shoulders and held me tight. I was terrified. And to add to my confusion he was whispering that he could help me get top marks, as a woman the other professors would give me low grades and he could help. He was on my side.

"He then pushed me over a table and tried to rape me. There was nothing subtle about his actions, and I tried to resist. I didn't know anything about self-defense. I was skinny and . . ."

She closed her mouth. Her shut eyes leaked tears. Alexander put his hands to his face. She turned her head toward him, then opened her eyes. "When he was through, I felt ashamed and guilty. I thought I was to blame. I don't know how I made it home.

"I look back and it's like I was a different person. I was utterly powerless. If I had reported him, I'd have been thrown out of med school. They would never have believed me. So I stayed in my room for days crying.

"I passed, barely. I never told a soul. Later, I heard he had tried the same thing on other students but we didn't talk about it back then."

Mel unclasped her hands and held Alexander's, squeezing them, as if using Morse code. Her eyes were focused on a spot on the floor.

"I searched for a karate class and tried several schools until I found a sensei who would treat me seriously. It's how I started."

Alexander kept still. She had her eyes closed again but did not withdraw her hands.

"I don't know why I deserve you," he said. "You're an amazing woman. Thank you for telling me. I don't know what to say, and I'm sorry I caused you so much pain recounting your story."

Mel raised her eyes to his face. "Those dimples," she whispered. "They always make me smile."

"Dimples?" He grimaced. "You don't trust men, do you?"

"Any more deep thoughts?"

"So you chose women's health as your practice. And you have me checking out a massage parlor operating as a brothel with an abusive maniac owner. Explains a lot."

"I can never tell when you're being insightful or just sarcastic."

"Oh, I have the same problem. But tonight I'm serious. Especially after the scare with him. I needed you there to protect me. You want to protect the people in your life who are threatened, as you were not protected when you were attacked."

"You don't know the half of it. I help run a women's refuge. It's a safe house. Been open since last year, but we might have to move it. Or get another house as well. Do you know what I'm talking about?"

"Battered wives can escape their dominating and violent husbands and stay in a safe house for a few days or weeks until they get their life back together. One's been running in Wellington for some time. And there's the hotline. What are you trying to do, anyway?"

"Find out why these women are scared and physically damaged. Who's doing it to them? Just one man or several? I thought it was obvious."

"Oh, I thought so too. It seems, apart from the drunken clientele, it's the owner who's the problem and what can we do about him? Especially if his workers choose to work there. I could talk to Inspector Grimble. He's my mate now, believe it or not."

"What would you say?"

"Tell him what I saw. It's enough for him to start an investigation, I think. Especially the two-way mirror."

"How would you explain you going there?"

"Can I use your name? Tell him you asked me to go? Check it out?"

"I don't think you should mention me."

Mel got up to make another pot of tea. There was a somber mood in the kitchen.

"Have you had a defining moment in your life where everything changed and you were set on a new path, a path you didn't have control of, but thought you had to follow because of what had happened to you?" Mel asked after she got the milk out of the refrigerator.

"It's how we become defined as human beings. Used to be childbirth for women and going to war for men, to make us who we are, our role in society. Went on for centuries, but it's gotten complicated now." Alexander said. "Don't think I'm having deep thoughts. We learned it in history at Grammar School."

"But for you? What happened to you?"

"I met you."

"No, silly. I'm serious—what happened to you?"

"I've never really thought about it till now, but I think it was being seduced by an older man who smoked a pipe, in his government office."

"You make it sound sinister. Was it sexual?"

"No. Political. It released something in me, something I find scary. The ability to work out solutions to problems I never knew existed. The willingness to do things I would never dream of in an ordinary life."

"Now you've lost me. What ordinary life?"

"I'm too tired to talk about it. Besides, coming back to you, I mean, I am gob-smacked, being with you, and what you told me about yourself. I'm glad you told me, and I hope we're closer. No?" Alexander wanted to kiss her, caress her.

Mel sat very rigid, her hands in her lap. He was waiting for a sign from her, a green light.

"Gob-smacked? The word you used to describe me when we first met?"

"Yes. The look in your eyes, the way you held yourself and threw your hair back and those Doc Marten boots. I always want to have that gob-smacked feeling around you. Astonished in a beautiful way." His eyes stayed on her face as they sat across from each other in the kitchen. "I could use the word spellbound if you like. Yes, spellbound."

"Spellbound? Like a witch?"

"No, spellbound as in magic. You are magic."

"And you, you always run your hands through your hair when you're nervous."

"I do?"

"Yes. You don't know?"

"I must always be nervous, especially around you."

"See, you're doing it again, and I love your longer hair."

"Ah. You finally noticed." Alexander resisted the impulse to ran his hands through his hair again. He kept his hands clasped on the table.

"I noticed when I picked you up at the airport. You were in too much of a rush to get me here." Her lips moved to a half-smile.

"So where are we now?" Alexander asked.

"Give me time. Be patient."

Mel stood and walked to her bedroom, leaving no doubt as to where Alexander was to sleep again.

CHAPTER TWENTY-TWO

"**D**id you think he would turn out so good?" The Minister held the black-and-white photos in his right hand.

"Well, I thought it was worth the gamble. If he failed, there was no downside to us." Richard Catelin smiled as he shifted his legs and adjusted the crease of his pinstripe trousers. He faced the Minister's desk, smaller than his own, and had to sit upright to see his boss. He kept his hands on his knees and saw the ashtrays were still missing. He could not bring out the pipe he had prepared.

"You thought he would fail?" The Minister looked displeased. His robust chest and matching stomach were neatly wrapped in a double-breasted pinstripe suit. He was menacing when he peered at Catelin. The legs of the chairs opposite his desk had been chopped two to three inches so their occupants felt smaller. The whole point of coming into his office, his official sanctum, the seat of power.

The Minister dropped the photos on his empty desk. "What are we going to do with these?" He stared at Catelin, who had the nerve to stare back.

"I think we should let the police do their job."

"Just watch out for Jarvis. I have no idea how he became superintendent. Before my time. I can't figure it out—maybe he had something on my predecessor. Idiots like that can be dangerous. It's a wonder he hasn't done more damage. Can you keep an eye on the situation, Catelin?

"Yes, sir. I'll see to it."

Catelin stood, reached for the photos and put them back in the envelope, before slipping them into his thin, leather briefcase. He knew how to keep things hidden. He left the office without a handshake or goodbye, as the Minister was already on the phone with another problem he had to deal with.

Richard Catelin, Permanent Under-Secretary in the Department of Internal Affairs, knew he would be around long after his current boss had lost his portfolio, either by scandal or election. Catelin was a civil servant and therefore, as his title implied, permanent.

$$. \qquad . \qquad .$$

"So delicious and moist." Michael wiped his mouth and chin, then licked his fingers.

His sister scowled at him.

"It's the gas oven. That, and the manuka honey."

"Yeah. Your best yet."

They sat at the counter in Barbara's large modern kitchen overlooking the rear garden.

Michael smacked his lips and reached for a third scone. Barbara hit his knuckles with a wooden spoon. "Don't want to spoil your figure. The girls at the Flamingo will notice."

"Reminds me, I got real good video of the arson insurance joker last night. Him naked in a bubble bath, all his insane comments. He couldn't stop talking."

"You mean Mr. Lance Beefeater himself?"

"Yes, in all his glory. Even got the happy ending. A hand job. Wish we could edit it in slow motion."

"You got the tape?"

"Of course. And I took some photos."

"Make copies. Here's what we're going to do. Call him. You have his number?"

"He filled it out at the counter."

"Set up a meeting tomorrow. Give him a copy of the tape. He has to approve all the Looks' and Wongs' insurance claims. It's been a year. Poor buggers deserve all their money. When the checks are in their hands, Beefeater gets the original videotape and photos. It's perfectly simple."

"Are you thinking what I'm thinking?"

"I hope so. We visit Bruce Look and tell him we're taking his entire crop. In fact, he has to deliver it to us."

"Sounds better. Their risk."

"They don't know what we know or what we don't know. They'll expect we do know. We'll give him an address and time, change it at the last moment and snatch the goods. They have two trucks, right? We saw them in the barn."

"And you're also thinking what I'm thinking about the trucks?"

Michael grabbed another scone and put it in his mouth before Barbara could hit him.

"We'll need more manpower." Barbara frowned. "Think you can arrange it?"

"Talking of checking names at the counter, there was a strange guy who came in twice. I saw him first in a car spying on the place. Goes by the name of Doug McLeish. Although he spelled it with an i before e last time. You know the union leader?"

"That old reprobate? At our place?"

"No. This guy's too young. He's not a cop. I can spot a cop a mile away and his phone number was wrong, so I don't know who he is or what he's doing, snooping around."

"You think he's working for someone else?"

"Don't know. Next time I see him we're going to have a little talk."

"Mikey, be careful and let me know. I like our little talks."

They both chuckled.

.   .   .

"The Minister likes the photos and wants to see a plan to take down the Maori gang and their illegal drug operation." The former Police Commissioner Ian Thompson held the black-and-white photos against the steering wheel. "As if we can ever win this war on drugs. There I go, talking in absolutes again."

Inspector Grimble, seated next to him, was feeling uncomfortable. Thompson had called the meeting at the golf course parking lot in the early evening. The lot was empty but for Grimble's Falcon and the commissioner's Riley. Grimble knew better than to make any comments while Thompson was speaking.

"Jarvis will be briefed. We don't want any leaks. Our aerial surveillance, all those fly-overs were wasted. How could we miss such a huge operation? We didn't know about it until that curator infiltrated them. There must be a truckload or two of drugs ready to come to Auckland. We can't go there without starting another Maori war, so we'll have to wait to snatch the truck or trucks when they come to Auckland. We don't want to try to seize them in some clearing in the bush. The cleaner the better. A roadside stop with lots of backup nearby, perhaps? Catch them green-handed, so to speak? Do you have any ideas?"

"Yes, sir. I've been thinking we need some light surveillance so we can monitor when the trucks are coming. We've circulated a photo of Wilson's car and a description and photo of the driver, but so far nothing. Which brings me to my next point—what if they don't use trucks but cars with smaller loads and hidden compartments. How do we stop them?"

"You're right. We always seem to think the criminal is going to do the same thing again. Even if it didn't work the last time. Rather than adapting to a new situation. Damn. We could have it all wrong. What does Alexander Newton have to say? Technically he's working for Catelin but he's keeping you informed of everything, right?"

"Yes. He briefed me first, sir."

"And no parking jokes."

CHAPTER TWENTY-THREE

When Alexander walked into the Auckland Central Police station in Cook Street he was wearing his navy blue suit, dark-red tie and white shirt. He was escorted to the elevator then into another office, not Inspector Grimble's. He inspected the cramped conditions, the piles of folders and papers as well as pins and labels stuck in maps of Northland and Auckland on the wall. There were Polaroids on one side of the map. He studied the display and recognized a few faces. To his relief, his own photo was not on the wall.

As soon as Grimble and Cadd walked into the room Alexander produced an envelope with a new set of black-and-white photographs. "I took these outside the Flamingo Paradise."

Grimble shot a glimpse at Cadd whose eyes were fixed on the out of focus Michael Donnelly at the front entrance, then asked, "What were you doing there?"

"Taking photos. Trying to find out what was happening to some of the girls. They're getting abused."

"And you found out how?" Cadd asked. "They're prostitutes. Goes with the territory."

"Well, not necessarily. I mean, it shouldn't go with the territory, should it? A friend asked me to dig around a bit to find out what was going on."

"And your friend is Dr. Johnson?" Grimble asked.

"I can't tell you and I hope you are discreet." Alexander saw he had their full attention. "You see, she's been treating young women for all sorts of unusual injuries. Not your normal 'night at the local sleazy massage parlor' sort of thing, so she wanted me to investigate the place. As you can imagine, none of the girls would ever dream of pressing charges or complaining." Alexander pointed to the telephoto shot of Michael Donnelly. "He's far too intimidating. They're genuinely scared of him. I bumped into him last night and I'm scared of him too."

"What happened?" Cadd asked.

Alexander told the story about the two-way mirror in room nine.

"The odd thing was I bumped into a strange country-bumpkin type last night in their sauna. He was called to room nine. Can't forget the name, Lance Beefeater. I think he was putting on an act. No one acts like such a country hick. And his name—is it real?"

Grimble pointed to the photos spread out on a table. "Can we keep these? What car did Beefeater drive?"

"An old black Mercedes. Four-door. And the boss drove a new black Jaguar XJ6. Nice car. I have photos of these." Alexander sorted out two photos from the pile.

The sergeant and the inspector looked at each other in silence.

Grimble said, "When Wiremu Wilson or whoever calls you about the shipment, call me immediately."

Alexander recited the inspector's number from memory. "What about the Flamingo Paradise?" he asked.

"Leave it to us. I don't want you going there again. It'll be too dangerous. He's Terry Turner's brother-in-law. We have our eye on him. He's ruthless. I have your word?"

Grimble held out his hand and Alexander gritted his teeth as he felt the inspector's tight grip.

.   .   .

Alexander walked from the Central Police station down Albert Street with his suit jacket slung over his shoulder. He turned right at Wellesley Street to enjoy the spectacle of his favorite cinema, the Civic. Planning new exhibitions, he wished to recreate his childhood sense of wonder being inside the Civic, with its mock open sky dome covered in twinkling stars, and the life-size panthers with blinking eyes on either side of the giant screen. He toyed with the idea of using the concept in his coming interview with the new director of the Auckland City Art Gallery. For the exhibitions curator position, Alexander wanted to pitch original ideas and feature local artists, both young and old, but thought he might overreach with the analogy of the Civic and its grandiose fantasy animals and Moorish designs.

At the corner of Wellesley and Queen Street he saw how vivid everything appeared in the Auckland sunshine. When the buzzer sounded, all traffic stopped and dozens of people crossed the giant intersection in all directions. Auckland seemed a happier and brighter place to him, big enough for a rich cultural life but not impersonal. Queen Street was more alive than any street in Wellington. Young men wore bell-bottomed trousers and loud shirts, while women were wrapped in miniskirts and vibrant blouses. Even the hippies and punks looked better dressed. He could live here again in the sunshine with cool evening breezes from the Gulf, and lazy afternoons lying under a tree in Albert Park. He had had enough of the high winds and constant storms of Wellington.

After the *Three Contemporary Maori Artists* show, his secret plan was to move to Auckland and be with Mel.

He stood outside the gallery entrance on Kitchener Street and thought about Mel and the story she told him last night. How could he win her back? And how much longer was he going to be sleeping on the sofa?

Whatever he had to do, it would have to be drastic and final.

.   .   .

Barbara stopped at the memorial to her husband Terry Turner, where the petrol station had been. She walked over to the black-marble edifice and saw that her flowers and card were no longer there. She adjusted her big blond wig and muttered something under her breath. She wore no make-up and appeared older, meaner.

"The devil you know," she repeated.

"What?"

"Nothing."

"No, you said something. It's bothering you." Michael faced her. "Out with it."

"Well." She sighed. "I not only lost my husband, I lost my lover. It's a big gap. You don't know how I feel. I feel sad. *Sad.*"

"And mad."

"Oh, yes. Mad. Mad for revenge."

Michael lifted his dark glasses and eyed the older Kingswood he had taken off the lot. He had a broad smile. "What's our plan, then?"

"Are you trying to be a teddy boy?" She glared at his black leather jacket and jeans.

"They've never seen me. Want to keep it that way. Especially if you're thinking what I'm thinking."

"Well, don't."

"What?"

"Think. It's dangerous."

"What *is* our plan? You don't want to underestimate them. Your late husband wasn't so clever, was he? Otherwise he wouldn't have been blown sky-high, along with John."

"John was sure to have thoroughly checked out the truck. They must've hid it real good."

"Means they're cleverer than Terry or John."

Barbara gave her brother a dirty look. "We'll have to be careful, but never underestimate the power of fear to motivate people."

"And money."

Barbara walked back to the Holden. Once she had started the V8, she said, "We go in there once we're sure it's only the two brothers, and I'll do the talking."

"We'll check it out from the hill? You have your binos?"

"They're yours."

"Oh yes. Shit, they're in my Jag. Anyway, we can see well enough from there."

"Terry used to say, the secret to being a good criminal is to make them fear you."

"If they haven't heard of your reputation, make 'em."

"But if we're in disguise how will they know who we are?"

"Fuck, Mikey. It's not complicated. Always keep your enemies guessing. If they fear you, they won't betray you. Because what do bad guys do?"

"They always fuck up and betray you. Show me a reliable criminal and I'll show you . . ." Michael moved his head to one side. "What did Terry used to say?"

"Fucked if I can remember. He was always carrying on. Fuck it, just make sure Chuck doesn't have explosives on him."

"Ha ha. Very funny."

.   .   .

They had kept Bruce Look's house under surveillance from the hill, until Barbara lost patience and drove to the front door, certain that only Bruce and his brother Chuck were there.

They barged their way into the living room. "Sit down!" Barbara commanded in a firm voice in contrast to her false smile. "Just a nice friendly chat. No need to overreact."

She stood in front of Bruce Look, who kept his mouth wide open. Chuck Look had tried to block the visitors, but Michael had pushed him onto the sofa, and smiled. The smile might not have been convincing but what got the Looks' attention was the silver revolver Michael held in his right hand. He brandished it in their direction, as if defying them to try anything.

"What are you doing here?" Bruce managed to say.

"Thanks for inviting us," Barbara began.

"You forced your way in!" Bruce shouted.

Chuck started to say something too but Barbara raised her hand. Then she looked at the walls and her mind went blank. Behind the sofa was a framed reproduction of *The Chinese Girl* with her blue-green face and cherry-red lips. On the other wall behind a matching sofa there was a framed painting of *Tina*, the wide-eyed buxom brunette with bare shoulders staring back at her. She could not wait to tell her best friend Beverly Jarvis about the two paintings.

She snapped back to see Michael wave his revolver at the surprised young men, obviously enjoying himself. She would have to talk to him about how he had acquired the revolver. Handguns were illegal in New Zealand and, as she had seen on their recent trip to Australia, men who carried handguns tended to use them.

She sneered at Bruce Look. "You have to listen to us. First, we've worked out a deal with your insurance adjustor, Lance Beefeater. You know him, right? He's now going to give you top dollar on all your claims. *All* of them."

She noted their shocked faces. "Are you listening?"

Bruce Look shook his head and glanced at the intruders, then his brother. "I don't understand. What's this got to do with you?"

"Everything, Bruce. Will you listen? Christ almighty. Let's begin again. My name is . . . Well, you know my name don't you? Barbara Turner."

She studied their reaction. The Looks stared at her, wide-eyed, speechless.

"Yes, my husband was Terry Turner, who you blew up. Only, the cops are too stupid to work that out. And you murdered John Eustace as well, who was a good friend of mine. But let's forget the past for now. I'm here on business." She paused to make sure her words sank in. "I'm going to let that go for now." Another pause, another scan of the room. "*If*, and it's a big if, you agree to my terms."

Bruce and Chuck sat side by side, frozen on the sofa.

"First, the good news. Beefeater is going to approve all your claims. All of them. The Hungry Wok, the motorcycle accident, Chuck's loss of earnings and all his medical bills. Good to see you're recovered now, Chuck."

"Thank you," Chuck muttered as he kept his eyes on Michael's revolver. "I think."

"Don't mention it. And you had an outstanding claim for a Volvo that mysteriously caught fire. Remember, Bruce? They never paid you for the car. The bastards. But now they're going to. Oh, and let's not forget Tony Look, and his death in the explosion. Even though they found no remains. The official report said he was at the Hungry Wok and his life-insurance policy, it's quite substantial, will be paid in full. I think Tony's widow will be happy, won't she, Bruce? Correct? I mean, the payout. It's not been good for her, has it?"

Bruce grimaced. The small woman with big blond hair who had appeared in his living room, unannounced, had a frightening authority. He was transfixed.

"Now, in return for all the money you're going to finally receive for all your losses, you're going to give us your entire harvest. Every bud, leaf and scrap, all packed and ready to be moved."

Bruce and Chuck exchanged a look.

"It's a sweet deal. We know you have the goods ready to ship. The sooner you offload it all, the sooner you'll be safe again. We have the police in our pocket. You think *you* do, but you don't.

"We have everything under control. We'll call you and give you instructions. And no explosives this time.

"You'll drive the truck to a location we'll tell you. And don't worry about Beefeater, he'll call you and tell you the good news himself. And you'll get it in writing. So you'll know it's true."

She paused, and Michael returned her impassive expression. "Do you understand what I've told you?"

"We're not giving up our harvest," Bruce whispered.

"Quite right, Bruce. We're giving you all the insurance money, money you would never get, ever. You realize that, don't you? The Hungry Wok was an act of vandalism not covered by your policy. Neither was Marty's death. Chuck's bike and Tony's supposed death by the explosion was caused by an illegal act. Two, actually. An act of war, with C-4, and the truck was full of illegal narcotics. And there's the Volvo, also an act of vandalism. So, in the real world, you would get nothing. You're criminals. Growers of illegal drugs. But now you're getting what?"

She turned to Michael, who said, "You should know the dollar amount, Bruce. All perfectly legal. You can take the checks to the bank and legally cash them or invest the money. It is legal and risk-free. All you have to do is deliver the goods to an address we'll give you by phone. You have nothing else to worry about."

Michael held the revolver behind his back as he scanned their astonished faces. For once, his smile was genuine. He was enjoying himself.

Barbara hesitated before she reached the front door then marched back to the living room and ducked behind the sofa, where the two Looks were still seated, astonished expressions on their faces.

"You won't be needing this, after you cash those huge checks. So I'll take it as a reminder of our little talk." She unhooked the framed painting and carried *The Chinese Girl* out of the house as Michael trotted to open the back door of the car. She carefully placed the painting inside.

As Barbara started the engine her brother looked back at the silent house, then turned to face her.

"You are one mean woman," he said admiringly.

Barbara Turner looked at her new acquisition resting on the back seat. *The Chinese Girl.* If she gave it to Beverly and her husband ever discovered where it came from, he would have a fit. She allowed herself a quick smile.

CHAPTER TWENTY-FOUR

"**W**e can't put a tap on Wilson's phone because he doesn't have one. And we can't have cars tracking any vehicles coming from their base. They'd notice, or one of our own would tell them. So we're going to keep the operation very close. Set up an undercover car just north of Orewa. The big hill before you get to Waiwera. They can stop any suspicious car and call in anything they find. Jarvis has approved the operation."

"Really? All the overtime?" They leaned over the map Cadd had spread over the inspector's desk.

"Yes. Cheaper than other options. He thinks it's his idea, so arrange it will you, Cadd? And while you're at it, work out something similar if they come down the west coast. They could turn east toward Dairy Flat or continue to Helensville, so we need to put a car somewhere north on State Highway 16, along the Kaipara Coast. Got it?"

"Yes, sir."

"But our best hope is actually Alexander Newton, much as I hate to admit it. When we find out about the five pounds, we can zero in on the delivery."

"If the five pounds even exists. Maybe Wilson did use it as a ploy to fool Alexander and by extension, us?"

"Let's go with the plan for now," said Grimble. "If there's no phone call in the next few days, we'll have to rethink our options. It makes sense to follow whoever delivers the package. If it comes. We'll give Alexander the money. It'll be marked so we can trace it later. But we do nothing with Alexander in the picture. I don't want him in any danger and it's unlikely Wiremu will personally deliver. What do you think?"

"Wiremu and Rawiri Wilson will be watching nearby. There's too much at stake. Could be a problem for any surveillance we plan."

"Yes, that's the challenge. How to outwit them. They're cunning. They'll be watching for us. I don't want the Drug Squad involved, for obvious reasons. Maybe as back-up but not nearby. They'll stick out."

"Agreed. We're going to need more manpower. All undercover. Will Superintendent Jarvis approve?"

"He'll have to. Thompson's still calling the shots."

"What about the other thing?" Cadd asked.

"Oh, yes. Curious, isn't it. We're looking at Barbara Turner and in walks Alexander with photos of her brother at the Flamingo Paradise and a possible blackmail deal with Lance Beefeater, whom we haven't gotten around to talking to yet. Get me the list of Turner's properties you created last year. I need to think about this very carefully."

.   .   .

Inspector Grimble had phoned Lance Beefeater in his glass-tower office off Queen Street. They arranged to meet at one of the oldest pubs in the city, tucked away in a narrow pedestrian mall called Vulcan Lane. Between Queen Street and High Street there were small cafes for the lunch and after-work drinks crowd, as well as two pubs and vintage-clothing and record stores.

The two policemen arrived early and found a high table in the cellar with a view of the stairs and entrance. It was too late for lunch and too early for dinner. There were only a few drinkers, older men permanently attached to the bar.

"Are you going to order a pint, sir?" Cadd asked.

"No. But let's encourage him to drink. We need him to talk—and talk of the devil, here he is."

A tall, thin man in a gray sharkskin suit surveyed the room before he walked to their table. They stood, shook his hand and introduced themselves.

"Crickey dick. This place has been around forever. Reckon those jokers at the bar were there when I was a student." He settled into a high seat and beamed at them "What an honor. Two of Auckland's finest. Whatever could I have done to deserve this?"

"It's what you haven't done we're interested in." Inspector Grimble knitted his brows and the insurance investigator froze, a little too dramatically for Grimble's liking.

"We've been meaning to talk to you for ages. You came highly recommended by everyone we spoke to. You know your stuff."

"Jeez. Thanks, mate. I mean inspector. Nice to be appreciated. How can I help you?"

"We understand that your company underwrote all the policies related to the Looks and the Wongs. Meaning you are, or were, investigating the arson at the Hungry Wok, the explosion on the Southern Motorway at the petrol station and the life-insurance claims too. Specifically, Tony Look and Martin Wong. Correct?"

"Yes. You have your information all accurate and such. Why the interest now? It happened a year ago. I put in requests for police reports back then. Never got back anything."

Grimble remained silent.

Beefeater squirmed in his seat.

"Are you here because of the visit I got the other day? From her?"

He looked at Grimble, then at Cadd, who both stared back at him without speaking.

"It's illegal and I think it stinks to high heaven. But if I tell you all about it, can you protect me? I mean, they are a nasty couple. Real nasty. I'm not Charles Bronson."

"Then tell us everything," Grimble shot back. He sensed that Beefeater would talk himself into cooperating, despite his unease, even without his first beer.

"What do you want to know?"

Grimble kept his eyes on Beefeater who appeared nervous. "Start from the beginning."

"I'm starving. I missed lunch and it's a long story. Let's order before it gets crowded."

"The fish and chips are good here. Beer batter." Cadd smiled. "And the kitchen's just opened."

Grimble told Cadd to order three fish and chips at the bar.

"So Lance, tell me. We're speaking man to man here, and it doesn't need to go further because it's not relevant to our other investigations, but we need to know. What happened?"

"Well, it's like this. I'm being blackmailed by Mrs. Turner, Terry Turner's wife, to write checks for all the claims the Look family have, and the Wongs as well."

Grimble glanced at Cadd. "Go on. What are the claims again?"

"Well, everything. It comes to rather a lot of money." Beefeater went on to itemize every claim both families currently had with his insurance company and how all the claims had been held up, for a variety of reasons.

"Could you approve all these claims?"

"That's just it. I can. I have the authority to approve them. Of course, my district manager and then his boss have to sign off too, but it's routine. They'll do so on my recommendation. They trust me. I've never made a mistake, a wrong move, so to speak. Until now." He lowered his head.

"Then I want you to go ahead and start the process to get them the checks," said Grimble. "They can be cancelled later. Even if they are written, you can stop them being cashed, right?"

"Yes, I can. I think. What do you have in mind?"

"Lance. You've trusted us and we can protect you. You've committed no crime. As far as I can tell. We need them to think they're getting the money. We'll do the rest. If anything happens at your insurance company, I'll personally come in and straighten it out. Okay?"

Beefeater nodded and looked ashamed.

"Lance. You're safe with us. Do you understand?"

"Yes, sir. Thank you."

Their plates of fish and chips arrived and Cadd went to order three beers from the bar, which was now filling up with the after work crowd.

.   .   .

"How come we've never heard of him before?" Cadd asked once Beefeater had left the pub. "I'd remember a name like that."

"Simple. All fire-insurance company requests have to be approved by the commander. In other words, Jarvis. I'm not involved."

They walked to High Street where Grimble had ille-gally parked his Ford with the blue light visible on the dashboard.

"Never knew that." Cadd burped. "And why didn't you bring him to HQ?"

"It was a friendly chat. When someone is being pres-sured like that, you can't force them to tell you what they've done. They're usually embarrassed, ashamed, you name it. At least out in the open, he did talk, didn't he?"

"But he didn't tell us *everything*."

"They never do the first time. We'll get the rest soon. We have more than we had before we met him. A lot more."

"Do you think it has something to do with the Flamingo and the two-way mirror?"

"Could be, but we don't need to speculate, do we? We know he's being forced by Mrs. Turner to commit fraud. The Looks have to hand over all the pot they've grown, so they'll get the insurance checks. It's the only logical expla-nation for Beefeater's blackmail."

"Oh, that's the connection. It was right in front of our eyes."

"Yes. What we need now are interception warrants for the Looks and Ricky Wong, based on our first-hand visit and of course intelligence from our ace Sergeant Bradshaw and what Beefeater told us. Then we need another warrant for Turner and her properties. We want to include the Flamingo Paradise and the car lot in Ellerslie, just down the road. I hear it features some high-priced cars now. You know the requirements for these, correct?"

Cadd nodded. He had kept copies of every warrant he had created or come across related to the 1961 Crimes Act. All he had to do was retype them.

"Should keep you busy the rest of the day, Cadd. I'll talk to Thompson. He'll prepare the judge we've used before. I hope you don't have plans tonight."

Grimble started the Ford. He had a new whiteboard he wanted to play with. He thought he was at a stage where he could map out all the players and see what relationships they had to each other. The Flamingo Paradise connection was an added bonus—if the curator from Wellington did not mess it up.

.   .   .

"It's a fucking nightmare! Not again. How can we have gotten into such a mess? How does she know?" Ricky pulled on his hair and eyed Bruce in disbelief.

"Hello, Ricky. How are you?" Bruce shot back with an edge to his politeness.

Ricky walked into Bruce's kitchen and helped himself to a beer from the refrigerator. "Where's Chuck?"

"Where do you think? Packing the harvest. Wants it all ready to go at a moment's notice. And the wife and kids are visiting Grandpa Sam."

"Are we going to go through with her deal?" Ricky asked.

"Whatever you call it—deal, blackmail, extortion—we get the check in the end."

"We have powerful allies."

"Everything has a cost, doesn't it? If we get Wiremu and his crew to help us, what will they want? Our entire crop? Half of it? Then we don't get the insurance money. If you add it all up, it's worth more than our crop. We would never get it otherwise. It's nice and clean. Into the bank, all accountable. And *legal.*" Bruce leaned against the sink and watched Ricky finish the beer. "Well, more legal than this."

"We need to get some assurances from the insurance guy, what's his name?" Ricky put the bottle on the kitchen table and wiped his mouth.

"Beefeater."

"We need to get paid for all our claims before we hand over the crop. Otherwise we'll be screwed—and then what do we do?"

Ricky belched. "Oh, I have a plan."

.   .   .

"I feel like we've been here before." Michael stretched back in the old Holden with the single front seat. He glanced at his sister who was gripping the steering wheel even though the engine was off and the brake was set.

"You're joking, right?"

"You can tell?"

"With you, I have my doubts," she hissed between her teeth. "Whatever happened to what's-her-name?"

Michael grunted. "Gave her money to get an abortion in Sydney then never heard from her again. Gratitude."

Barbara glared at him with her unblinking Cleopatra eyes. "Good riddance. I thought you might have . . . You know."

Michael ignored her taunt and checked the mirrors. The street was quiet with only a few people walking by. No one seemed to pay them any attention.

"What do we do once we know she's there? You're not thinking what I'm thinking, are you? I mean, it's risky here in broad daylight." He saw a Pacific Island family sitting on their porch near where they were parked. "If you think she's a gift for me, thank you. But what's the point? And she has links to us from the Flamingo. Correct? If she disappears, it'll come back to us. There has to be another way."

"I was thinking of a little talk. Find out what she knows about her cousins in Pukekohe. Maybe we can keep her as a hostage. Until we get the entire shipment."

"I'm not babysitting her. And who says we need her? Isn't the videotape enough? Mr. Beefeater will deliver. It'll just complicate things. Didn't dear departed Terry say, 'Keep it simple, sweetheart'?"

"Don't take my beloved husband's name in vain. He was a lot smarter than you."

Barbara gave him another filthy look. After a long silence she said, "I still want her dead. She was responsible for my husband's death. It's only fair she dies as well. And at your hands. You'll enjoy it, won't you? Besides, we need something to scare those Chinese buggers into handing over their harvest. I still think they're scheming how to get out of the deal, even if they get the insurance money. I don't trust them. Bloody Chinks."

Michael ground his teeth. "You're not the jaded widow, you're the *evil* widow. So are we going to do it now or not? We know her husband's at rehearsal. We saw him leave with his violin."

"I've just had my nails done, and don't want to ruin them."

.　　　　.　　　　.

"I've put Barbara Turner in the middle with her brother Michael. Lance Beefeater is on the right here, and the Looks and Ricky Wong are over here on the left. Then we have Wiremu Wilson and his lot on the bottom center and I'm going to have to add Alexander Newton here at the bottom. We'll just call him the curator for now. Do you see all the connections we know of, so far?" Inspector Grimble stepped back and admired his whiteboard. He had photos of all his suspects, their names beneath them, and different colored lines connecting them.

"Why the red lines?" Cadd asked.

"I've only got two color pens I can wipe off the board."

Cadd tried not to laugh. Grimble's jaw was set and he seemed to be mesmerized by the names.

"We've got two ins. Beefeater and the curator. Beefeater will do exactly what we want, but I don't trust Newton because he has political backing."

"What do you mean?"

"He befriended Wiremu Wilson. We don't control him, as he's taking orders from Catelin and former Commissioner Thompson, who's reporting to the Minister. Catelin is the highest civil servant in the department and, like his title implies, permanent. Thompson is the former Commissioner, but still active here. He has the ear of the Minister and is out of our chain of command, which leaves us out on our own. If Newton screws up, we'll get blamed. If he's successful, they'll take all the credit. I don't care where the credit goes, but I do mind being exposed and having no control. We'll have to keep a close eye on Newton."

"It's what you said, cop politics," said Cadd. "And you're not going to name it Operation Mary Jane, as we discussed?"

"I think naming it will jinx the whole operation. Better we keep it under wraps. I've got a feeling things aren't going to go the way we expect and we'll either be outwitted, misled or internally subverted."

"Now you've lost me."

"Well, Cadd, you didn't even mention Superintendent Jarvis and *his* role. It's what you said, cop politics." He took a step back from the board and leaned on his desk. "We need to get Beefeater in here, and have him call the Looks. We can record it and that'll be a start."

Cadd went to his desk to call the insurance investigator.

.   .   .

Wiremu and Rawiri had driven to Auckland from their Hokianga base in another old Holden, to meet Ricky at his house and sort out a few locations for dropping off their product. The brothers had agreed they had to split their deliveries from Northland into smaller loads and avoid trucks and vans.

The scarred landscape of Grafton Gully felt much the same to Wiremu as he parked a few doors from Ricky's house and watched the passing cars, and the windows of the few remaining older Edwardian two-story houses in their scruffy glory.

Ricky greeted them at the door and scanned the street as if he was expecting surveillance. He ushered them back to the small kitchen. Dishes were piled high in the sink and the tap dripped. Wiremu thought that Ricky looked worried. Rawiri went straight for the bread bin.

"Where's Moana?" Ricky asked. "I thought she was coming too."

"Nah," Wiremu said. "Want to make sure it's all running right."

Rawiri cut a thick slice of Connons whole-wheat bread and slathered it with a knife-load of butter followed by manuka honey.

"You got the first delivery, right?" Wiremu asked.

"Yes. What a mad bugger. Your cousin told me to tell you he went to Gisborne for a while. He took a large bag with him."

Wiremu laughed. "Good on him. He's a smart bloke but probably a little stoned now."

"A *little*?" Rawiri said through a mouthful of bread.

"Genius hiding place. It's all gone. I'll have all the money by tomorrow at the latest. There's a huge demand." Ricky went to put the kettle on for tea.

"Good." Wiremu watched Rawiri consume a honey sandwich in a couple of mouthfuls. He had not told Ricky of all the other deliveries taking place in Coatesville and further south of Auckland.

"There is one complication, though," Ricky said. "But it doesn't concern you guys. More a family problem. Barbara Turner has demanded our entire crop in Pukekohe in return for our getting paid on all our insurance claims. All of them. The insurance company, the bastards, were never going to pay. Ever. It's a neat trick and blackmail all rolled into one. I'm still thinking about it."

Rawiri spat out a piece of bread and slapped the table. "Holy shit! Do you want us to take care of her?"

Ricky raised his eyebrows. "Do you realize what you're saying? You'd go to war against Barbara Turner?"

"They're our competition. And they sell heroin to our people. Not nice at all." Wiremu watched Rawiri to gauge his reaction.

Rawiri stopped chewing. "You want to do that? After what we talked about?"

"And then there's her brother," Wiremu said thoughtfully. "Are we just talking or are we planning? There's a difference."

CHAPTER TWENTY-FIVE

"I'd like to think we'll have all the warrants in place by tomorrow morning and we can start listening in. We also have the undercover and patrol cars further north briefed on what they need to be on the lookout for, including any of Wilson's known associates and their cars. You've got the Turner list?"

"There's the used-car lot down the road from the Flamingo Paradise. We haven't investigated it yet. It's got a garage, really a big workshop. And lots of cars. Expensive cars," said Cadd, standing by his desk with an odd expression.

"Good work. We need to visit the lot, soon," said Grimble. "But what's the matter, sergeant?"

"What if we're too late and everything's already in motion? All we've got is Beefeater's phone call to the Looks. I've got a feeling we're not ahead, we're behind."

"We need to eat. What is it, ten? Do you fancy the White Lady?"

If they had to work through the night, they would visit the White Lady, an open white bus parked on Commerce near Queen Street that served peas, pies, burgers, and pud, followed by a soda or coffee, and open till four in the morning.

The phone rang on Grimble's desk. Cadd flinched.

"Grimble speaking." He stared intently at his sergeant as he listened to the caller. Then he slammed the phone down. "Damn and blast. Bloody hell!"

It was the first time Cadd had heard his superior swear, and he looked suitably shocked.

"There's been a murder in Ponsonby. They're holding Clovis Tibet as a suspect. We need to get there now."

·   ·   ·

A traffic police car blocked the entrance to Lincoln Street, its flashing red light bouncing off the glass in the shop windows on Ponsonby Road. Another traffic police car blocked the road further down the street. Grimble parked by the traffic car with his blue light on and walked to the small cottage behind a white picket fence. A constable stood guard outside. There were Pakeha couples on their verandas nearby as well as families of Polynesians. The sergeant and the inspector marched inside to find a constable standing to one side of the living room. Clovis Tibet was bent over the body of Plum Blossom. Blood stained the wooden floor and soaked into the cracks. A large kitchen knife was next to the body. All they could hear was the wailing of Clovis, a giant man with a well-trimmed beard and short ginger hair, covered in blood.

"I couldn't get him off, sir, so I waited for you. Didn't want to disturb the evidence." The constable's eyes were still bulging at what lay before him. "You can see what state he's in."

Cadd and Grimble stood in the doorway and scanned the entire room before turning their attention to Clovis Tibet.

"He told me his name and who his girlfriend is, then he continued wailing. The neighbors heard and called

111. I was the first to arrive and my sergeant called you, inspector."

Grimble told Cadd to stay there. He walked very slowly through the small cottage and could see no broken windows or forced door jambs.

.   .   .

Alexander parked the same Hillman near the Flamingo Paradise. He had his Rollei 35 camera in his pocket but left the rest of his gear in the trunk. He had no idea how he could smuggle the camera into the room with the bathtub. In his initial surveillance he had seen no sign of the owner or his black Jaguar. He had left a note in Mel's mailbox for her to call Grimble's 24-hour phone number if he did not return by two o'clock. *I have to go back there.* He had scribbled on the card.

He watched and waited. When he felt it was the right time to enter, he slipped in behind a group of men walking into the massage parlor.

The two young women at the front desk signed him in after the other men had received their towels and keys to their lockers. The men had taken a long time deciding on the menu, with lots of guffaws, nudges, and backslaps, no doubt lubricated by their alcohol-fueled courage. Alexander went for everything, including the bubble bath. He left his Rollei in the locker.

Doug McLeish entered the packed sauna wrapped in his small white towel and his locker key on a band around his wrist. Sweat began to seep into his eyes, and his nostrils were assaulted with garlic and beer. He was in for a long night.

.   .   .

An hour later Grimble and Cadd were back at Central. Grimble had called Superintendent Jarvis to tell him of the possible arrest.

Jarvis was all for booking Tibet immediately, with no further interrogation. "There's no forced entry you say, so it has to be him. He's covered in blood and his fingerprints are probably on the knife. Wrap it up and write it up. We've got more important things to do with this big drug shipment, Grimble. Don't go all cowboy on me again."

The superintendent's phone call inspired Grimble to dig further. He did not want the case to unravel in court, or in the press, because he had not been thorough enough. He asked for forensics to go over the house again and report immediately to him in person. Other police were canvassing the neighborhood for any suspicious men seen near the house earlier in the evening.

The two detectives walked into the interview room and sat opposite a subdued Clovis Tibet. Forensics had issued him white paper overalls and removed his original clothes at the house. He still had blood on his face and hands. Tears dripped onto the table, stained with red whirls.

Grimble introduced himself and his sergeant, though he had no idea what Clovis had understood. He had been read his rights when he was placed in the chair but he had no handcuffs on. He looked bewildered.

"We first met when Plum Blossom went missing. About a year ago. Remember?" Grimble waited for a reaction but Clovis failed to respond. "I know you're in shock, Clovis. I would be too. We talked to Plum recently and were going to talk to you. Can you tell us what happened tonight? Take your time."

The detective's patience was rewarded when Clovis blinked, shook his head and started to talk. He told the same story again, slower, with frequent interruptions to wipe his eyes or suppress a sob. He had arrived home after rehearsals, a little after ten. The front door was locked and as he walked into the main room he saw Plum lying on her back. He did not see blood until he saw his boots were in a dark red lake.

A knife was nearby and yes, he had picked it up and run through the house thinking the intruder, the murderer was still there, but he wasn't, so Clovis dropped the knife back where he found it. Then he collapsed and held her. He knew she was dead and there was no point in trying to revive her. But he tried to shake her, grabbed her shoulders and when she did not respond, he hugged her as if willing her to come alive for him. When he finally realized she was dead, he had started to cry, then scream. Loudly.

This confirmed what the neighbors, who had called the police, had said. Grimble and Cadd had witnessed how blood had seeped into his clothes and where the knife was.

There was a knock on the door and Cadd went to open it. Grimble expected Forensics, instead it was a constable, who appeared very pale.

"There's been a fire, sir. In Pukekohe. A Sergeant Bradshaw said to contact him immediately. Something to do with the Looks' property, I think. And one more thing . . ."

Grimble eased out of the interview room to the corridor where the constable whispered, "Drug Squad just stopped a truck full of marijuana on the hill next to Orewa. But the two Maoris in the truck were not Ngapuhi, and they have no known connection to Wiremu Wilson. Superintendent Jarvis wanted you to know."

"See that Mr. Tibet here gets whatever he wants, a hamburger, a cup of tea, whatever," Grimble ordered. "Stay with him until we come back." As they left, Clovis had a confused expression on his bloody face.

"Didn't the constable say we had to contact Bradshaw?" Cadd asked as they waited at the elevator.

Grimble shrugged. "Part of me doesn't want to call him based on what he did last time. But . . ." He returned to his office to call the sergeant.

·   ·   ·

Alexander was relieved to be called to room nine. He felt dizzy from the heat and the procession of sweaty men with body odor who waddled into the sauna, making inane comments, or laughing loudly at their own jokes. He retrieved his Rollei camera from his locker and snatched a towel lying on the floor. With his back to the locker room door he extended the lens tube and adjusted the dials for exposure and aperture until he estimated where the needle for the light meter would be in the center. He thought he had enough light for the fast Tri-X film he had set for 800 ASA, and was confident he could steal a few shots to show Grimble. He then wrapped his Rollei inside the towel in such a way he could point the towel roll and shoot what he saw. He had his left hand inside the towel holding the camera and with his fingers he could cock the shutter, take a shot then wind the camera again.

Moans, loud voices, and muffled whispers came from different rooms. He wandered through the corridors and identified an emergency exit at the back of the house, and thought it would be alarmed. Past room nine he came to the hidden door. There was no one else in the corridor. He listened and, with his towel pointed forwards, leaned against the door so it would spring open. The tiny space was completely dark but for the window displaying a bathtub and a skinny blond bending over to adjust the water. There was a video camera on a tripod aimed at the bathtub. He took a photo of it and closed the hidden door, checking it had shut properly before he headed to room nine.

The corridor was empty as he advanced the film, the camera hidden in the towel. He knocked. The young woman introduced herself as Tiffany, and did not recognize Doug from Wellington.

Alexander turned to the mirror and squeezed the shutter as he asked Tiffany if she wanted him to remove his towel.

"Make yourself comfortable," she offered in a flat response. He could not tell who was more on edge, Tiffany or himself.

He placed the towel with his camera in a dry corner and dropped the other towel over it. He made an act of admiring himself naked in the mirror as he stepped into the tepid bathwater. Tiffany kept her towel on as she started to rub his back with a cold, wet cloth. He concentrated on listening for anything unusual from the other rooms.

Tiffany made a lather over his back then his front. There were few bubbles in the bath and Alexander felt helpless, unable to elicit a smile from Tiffany, let alone gather information about what was happening elsewhere in the massage parlor.

.   .   .

Grimble kept to the outside lane on the Southern Motorway, and made record time, his flashing blue light on the roof above the driver's side. They spotted Sergeant Bradshaw's new yellow vehicle at the Drury turnoff and caught up with a Papakura fire truck with its lights flashing and siren blaring. They formed a procession to the Looks' house.

"Why is he not in a police car, Cadd?"

"Don't know, sir. Want me to ask him?"

"Yes, when you get a chance."

When they arrived, two fire engines were parked far from the house in the valley. Hoses ran in every direction and a swarm of firemen and police were illuminated by flashing red and blue lights, headlights and spotlights. Large tire tracks and fire boots had ploughed through the neat rows of lettuces behind the house. The smoldering remains of a large shed and a partially burned tree in a grassy hollow were out of sight from the four greenhouses Grimble and Cadd had surveyed days before.

Grimble was still running through his head all the pictures he had stored of the crime scene in the small house on Lincoln Street, and the sight of Plum Blossom.

The Looks' cars were missing from the driveway. Bradshaw's utility was parked in front of the Ford. Grimble took a deep breath and prepared himself for the new crime scene he was about to inspect as he walked around what looked like a dark and deserted house. He followed Bradshaw, and Cadd jogged down the hill to catch him, trying not to step on the lettuces.

"All doors and windows are locked and no sign of any forced entry, sir," he reported.

A fireman directed the Papakura truck to where it was needed down the valley behind the house, across rows of destroyed vegetables. A distinct acrid pong came from the remains of the fire, along with the occasional popping sound of glass jars exploding. There was no available water and the original two trucks from the Pukekohe Fire Brigade had run dry. Firemen unraveled additional hoses to where dirty smoke rose from the remains of the structure.

Sergeant Bradshaw motioned for Grimble and Cadd to come closer. They could feel the heat and inhaled the distinct smells. The fire chief strode over in his protective gear and introduced himself to Grimble. "Do you know these people?" he asked.

"Yes. They grow vegetables." Grimble waved his hand over the destroyed crop they were standing on. "What did you find?" Grimble did not want his new ally to jump to conclusions too soon.

"It appears to be arson. An accelerant was used around the wooden structure and it must have ignited rapidly. There was a lot of dried inflammable material inside and glass. Looks like pot. But we'll have a better idea in the morning when everything's cooled off. I think half my men are stoned."

"No bodies? Nothing else damaged?"

"Can't see any, but we haven't gotten inside yet." He pointed in the direction of the house. "At least we saved that."

"Anyone inside?" Grimble asked.

"No, and no cars outside either."

"We'll talk in the morning. Thank you, chief."

Grimble turned to Bradshaw, who was standing close by. "What do you think, sergeant?"

"Just got here, sir."

"How did you hear about this?"

"Got a phone call at the station. That's when I called you, inspector."

"Anything else? Why aren't the Looks here?"

"I think they went to the hospital. I heard that an ambulance was called to Sam Look's house, earlier, on the radio. I could go see them."

Grimble turned to stare at Bradshaw. "Good idea, sergeant. And call in your report as soon as possible to Cadd. We have to get back to Auckland."

Grimble headed to his car and Cadd trotted behind him, leaving Bradshaw with his mouth wide open.

. . .

"Can you add some hot water? It's getting a bit cold." Alexander almost said he was shrinking, but as Doug from Wellington, he was on his best behavior. He needed Tiffany to confide in him. He was running out of time and wanted to have something to report back to Mel.

Tiffany poured hot water into the bath and dribbled some liquid from an unmarked plastic bottle, creating only a handful of bubbles.

"I feel like I'm on camera. With the big mirror there. There's not a camera behind there, is there, Tiffany? Tiffany?" He half-turned to catch her frozen. "I'm just joking. Hell, after a few beers everything seems funny. Know what I mean? What's with the face?"

"Don't say things like that here. It's not cool."

"Oh. I get it. I'll be cool. Just don't get to go to places like this where I come from. It's a treat. Can you do my lower back again, please? Right down there. Yes, perfect. Thank you, Tiffany. You've got great hands." He turned to smile at her and gauge her reaction.

He had miscalculated how frightened she was. "I'm thinking of moving to Auckland," he said quickly. "What's the best suburb to live in?"

He waited for a response. She squeezed the wet sponge she was using, over his head. "Like, where do you live? I mean, the suburb or whatever it's called? I've seen Epsom, it's cool."

"Yeah. Epsom's cool. Expensive, though."

Doug from Wellington tried to rub the weak soap out of his eyes. He ran his hands through his hair before leaning back again. "What about further south, like Onehunga or One Tree Hill?"

"They're good too." She now concentrated on his chest but went no lower than his belly button. Alexander rested his hands on top of the bathtub. He kept blinking then closed his eyes, hoping the pain from the soap would go away

"So where do you live, Tiffany, if I may ask?"

"We can't talk about that here."

"Oh. Sorry. Don't want to get you into trouble. I don't want your address, just an area you could recommend I could live."

He heard the door open. Tiffany's eyes bulged and her body stiffened.

·　　　·　　　·

Grimble drove back faster. The Southern Motorway was deserted but for a few long-distance trucks. He had the blue light attached to the roof on the driver's side. For some reason his side window could not close with the cord in place, unlike on the trip to Pukekohe.

"Who burned the Looks' crop?" Cadd had to shout over the noise from the window. "Do you think Bradshaw is guilty? I mean, he was evasive?"

"I'm not sure he was at the station if he met us with his own vehicle," said Grimble. "And if he heard about the ambulance, why didn't he hear about the fire also? On the police radio, I mean. What he said doesn't make sense."

"Let's hope the grandfather, Sam Look, is okay. I like the old man," said Cadd. "And whatever happened to him, was it before or after the fire?"

"We're going to find out. Check the radio call Bradshaw told us about and its time. Also what happened at the hospital. I also want to know who turned up there. And check with the desk sergeant in Pukekohe if Bradshaw was there. If they even have a desk sergeant. Looks like you'll have to go back there and talk to Bradshaw again. Like you're mates."

"Yes, sir. So who do you think set the fire?"

"Just about everybody is a suspect at the moment. I'll wait for the report. We have a cast of characters. Maybe Wilson did it to eliminate their competition—with no high-quality pot on the street, their prices would go up. Maybe Bradshaw, as part of some shakedown he had planned? What about Beefeater? He knows arson. And he wanted to get out of being blackmailed. Although I don't see what burning down the crop would accomplish for him. He still has all the other claims to pay out."

"How would Beefeater know about the Looks' crop? No one's told him, have they?"

"Good point. He can't know anything about the crop."

"No, sir. But you're forgetting one name, sir."

Grimble glanced at his sergeant. "Who?"

"Alexander Newton. The curator. What if he got orders to stir things up, destroy one whole crop, set them all against each other? When you think about it, it's brilliant, isn't it?"

"Oh, Cadd. Even I would never have dreamed of such a plot. But one thing I will wager, and I've never done it before. The person with the best alibi will be my top suspect."

"I'm betting they all have iron-clad alibis."

"Back to Clovis Tibet. What do you think of him? You haven't voiced your opinion, Cadd."

"You taught me well, sir. I don't have enough information to come to any conclusion yet. I'd like to see the Forensics report. Maybe we missed something. I can't imagine that having gone through so much with Plum Blossom, he'd then kill her. Doesn't make sense."

"I have news for you, Cadd. Most murders don't make sense." Grimble slowed down then accelerated through a red light, the blue light working.

"Who supplied the drugs on the truck from Northland? A new group we don't know about?" Cadd thought aloud as they came to Cook Street in downtown Auckland again.

"Yes. Curious indeed. Wouldn't it be just Wiremu Wilson's luck to get away with offloading his entire crop before we can catch him."

"Now more valuable than ever," Cadd mused.

"What else can go wrong tonight, Cadd?"

Cadd shook his head and kept quiet.

Grimble parked outside Central in front of a police van on the corner of Vincent and Cook Street.

Cadd said, "I suppose we won't be getting a pie at the White Lady?"

.   .   .

Alexander used both hands on the side of the dirty bathtub to give himself some traction as he concentrated on standing. Halfway up he was hit on the head, hard. He fell back into the bath and his head struck the edge of the bathtub.

When he came to, he was on the floor of a moving vehicle, naked and shivering wet. His arms and legs were bound. He sensed the van back into something. The engine died. He could not make out the location but heard large doors opening. Then the rope around his feet was pulled hard and he went flying out of the van onto concrete, hitting his head again.

He tried to move and blacked out.

.   .   .

"Did you buy Plum Blossom flowers?" Grimble asked as he and Cadd walked into the interrogation room again. He held a folder in his left hand.

"No." Clovis uncovered his face and shook his head. "Plum hated cut flowers. She liked them in the garden. I never bought her flowers."

"Had anything odd happened earlier?"

"No. I just went to my rehearsal at the usual time."

"When?"

"About five. I like to get there early. I take a leisurely walk across town. It relaxes me." He shrugged then covered his face with his hands again as he fought back tears.

In the time Grimble and Cadd had left him, someone had taken him to a bathroom to clean him. The paper overalls looked wet and stained but his face and red hair were free of blood.

"I know you're trying to help," said Grimble, "but think again. Did anyone call you earlier in the week?"

"I don't usually get calls. But, yes, we got a couple. Plum took them. She said they were wrong numbers."

"What about this afternoon?"

"Well, I did speak to a guy who called, name started with a B, maybe a Burt?"

"Yes?"

"He said he had just joined the orchestra and played the French horn. I knew we were having difficulty with our horn section, so I believed him. He wanted to know what time the rehearsal began. I told him six. Then he asked if the rehearsal went on longer than eight and I said they usually end after nine. He hung up right away, didn't even thank me or anything."

"And you didn't buy Plum Blossom flowers?"

"No. I told you she hates them. Did you see any flowers in the house? Any vases or jars for flowers?"

Grimble looked at Cadd, who nodded, agreeing with Clovis.

"You're right. There were no vases in the house. Then you wouldn't know why a white lily, actually a petal from a white lily, was found near the front door?"

"No," Clovis sighed. "I have no idea."

.   .   .

"I have someone you'd like to meet, dear little sister. For a little talk."

"Not on the phone, stupid. Where are you?"

"The usual place."

"Christ. It's late. Don't do anything. I'm coming over. Understand?"

Michael had switched on the lights by the side door. Only a few of the fluorescent tubes warmed up and flickered as he walked back to the dark area where the body lay. He took a large metal hook, tucked it into the knot wound around the feet and started to winch the body upwards.

His captive had regained consciousness, suspended upside down, and started to move his head.

Michael took the camera he had found in room nine out of his pocket and played with the aperture and exposure to get the light meter display in the center. He was familiar with the Rollei and by looking through the viewfinder he managed to compose a decent photo of the bloodied body of Alexander flailing around, his hands, unable to grab anything or touch the floor. Michael put the camera in his pocket and walked to Alexander. Timing his shot, he punched the suspended figure in the head with his right fist followed by a left hook in the ear. Both blows sent Alexander swinging back and forth.

Michael waited until the body became still. He took a piece of rope from his other pocket and tied the victim's hands again, very tightly, with an intricate knot. He took a few steps back and produced the Rollei again.

"Come on baby. Open your legs. Oh, that's right, you can't." He laughed under his breath, then realized he probably moved the camera as he pressed the shutter release, so he advanced the film. He held his breath, kept the camera steady and took another shot of his immobile model.

.   .   .

"Inspector Grimble? Thank heavens I found you. Alexander Newton left me your phone number and said I was to call you if something went wrong."

"Dr. Johnson? What's happened?" Grimble was about to take Clovis Tibet to a nearby hotel. He had to wait for the autopsy report to confirm the time of death and whether Plum Blossom had been sexually assaulted. The state of the body made it difficult to see any bruises or cuts. Grimble estimated that Plum Blossom had died before Clovis had returned. And whoever had killed her had talked his way into the house with a bouquet of white lilies. Every flower shop in Auckland would be questioned in the morning about the lilies. And he would task Cadd to ascertain if there was a new player named Burt in the orchestra's horn section.

"It's Alexander. He's missing. He went back to the Flamingo Paradise. I told him not to, but he hasn't returned and it's past two o'clock. They'll be closed now."

"Where are you?"

"At home."

"Stay there. We're on our way. Don't go looking for him."

He called to Cadd who was holding a tracksuit for Clovis to wear instead of paper overalls. "Quick, leave him. We'll be back, Mr. Tibet. To the car, Cadd."

.   .   .

Mel ran to her BMW, made a fast U-turn and roared to Mount Eden Road. She swerved left onto Stokes Road then Owens Road, and before she knew what she was doing, she was at Manukau Road. She flung the car onto Broadway through a red light and aimed for the Flamingo Paradise.

The neon sign was off. The house was dark. There were no cars parked outside. She left the engine running and banged on the front door but got no reply.

She turned and saw a small figure trying to slip past her from a side entrance.

"Hey you! Yes, you. Come here!" Mel yelled.

The young woman froze.

"It's okay." Mel gestured to placate her. "My name is Dr. Mel Johnson." Then the tone of her voice changed. "Tiffany? Is that you?"

"Yes," Tiffany managed to admit.

Mel came out of the shadows. "I just want to know if you saw a tall young man with longish brown hair tonight. Goes by the name of . . ." Her mind went blank as she looked into the young woman's frightened eyes. "Doug. Yes, Doug. Did you see him?"

Mel wanted to grab her by both arms, instead she showed her open palms and pleaded. "Tiffany, he's my boyfriend and he's in danger. Something's happened to him. You must've seen something. I don't want you involved but you've got to give me something to go on. *Please.*"

Tiffany opened her eyes wider. "Oh, it's you."

"Yes, I'm your doctor. Remember? You have to tell me where he is. That man has taken him somewhere, hasn't he?"

Tiffany took a deep breath. "Follow me. I'll point out where he might be." She walked across the road to her car, a dark VW Beetle. Mel rushed back to her BMW and followed Tiffany along Great South Road. The VW slowed and a hand pointed out the window to the car lot opposite. Then the VW sped off.

·   ·   ·

A small fence separated the lot from the street where Mel came to an abrupt stop. She switched off her engine but kept her hazards on. She eased her way through the unlocked gate and stood for a moment to survey her surroundings. There were two rows of cars with "for sale" signs, and what looked like a sales room to one side, then at the rear of the lot a large single-story structure with two closed roller doors. A Mercedes coupe and a van were parked in front. She could hear nothing, nor see any lights or signs of a night watchman.

She ran to the white van and placed her hand on the hood. It was still warm. Stepping around the building she saw a faint light from underneath the closed side door. She pressed her ear to the door and heard a scream. She knew how Alexander could scream, but not like this, high-pitched and in pain.

Mel wrenched the door open and charged into a dimly lit space. She stepped to one side to look around her. A woman in high heels, with jet-black hair tied back, held a cattle prod to Alexander. He screamed. The woman with the prod turned to see the intruder, then jabbed Alexander again. He was naked and suspended from a hook attached to his bound ankles. A solid-looking man in a blue shirt and khaki trousers stood to one side with a camera. Mel could make out his broken nose and cauliflower ears as he turned to snarl at her.

There was a car on a lift nearby, and other equipment she could not identify, and a large X-shaped cross leaning against the far wall. Only a few fluorescent lights worked: some of the tubes buzzed on and off, giving the space a macabre glow.

Mel ran to the menacing figure, who was nearer. The man looked at her in disbelief. She launched a front kick into his chest and as he stumbled she followed with a palm strike under his chin. He dropped the camera, lost his balance and fell backwards before Mel could hit him again.

The woman screamed at Mel and rushed toward her with the cattle prod. Mel advanced on her but at the last second stepped to her left, missing the prod aimed at her. She side-kicked the woman's right knee, knocking her to the floor. Mel leaped on her, grabbed the cattle prod and pressed the end into the woman's neck with as much force as she could manage. There was a searing sound then the smell of burnt hair before the prod died. The woman's body went into spasms and Mel kicked her head as hard as she could in her Doc Martens.

Mel grabbed the prod and tried to get it to work again but it was broken. She threw it at the enraged man who stared at her. The prod bounced off his chest. Blood dripped from his face.

Mel wanted to get Alexander down from the hook and check that he was still alive. Instead she had to deal with the man with cauliflower ears. She charged him again. He was ready and side-stepped her, holding his hands up protectively. He grabbed her right leg as she mistimed a roundhouse kick to his head. Mel lost her balance and hit the concrete but broke her fall with her arms spread out. She rolled on the floor as he held onto her foot.

On her back she tried to kick the man's grip on her ankle by using her left foot as a hammer. The force of the Doc Marten boot dislodged his hold on her ankle but as he managed to grab her again with more force, he pulled off her boot. He fell on his back. She rolled onto him and grabbed his right wrist, bent the wrist backwards and twisted it as she used her legs to propel herself in the opposite direction, away from him. She continued to bend his wrist toward his own body as she eased herself upwards. He gritted his teeth and used his superior strength to go with her momentum, but she used her full body leverage and sudden change of direction to keep him on the ground in a solid arm lock. He continued to struggle but she applied extreme pressure as she stood and leaned with greater force into him as he tried to escape the lock. She hyperextended his elbow and with all her force jerked his arm when she sensed she could not press it back further. There was a loud popping sound.

He swore through clenched teeth. She kept hold of his useless arm, pushed it further back and felt his clavicle break. She did not let up, such was her anger. So intent was she on destroying him she did not hear his screaming obscenities, nor his high pitched yelps of pain. Still holding the useless wrist, she stomped on his knee as hard as she could with her other boot. She heard another crack. He screamed even louder.

She discarded his limp wrist, stepped away and spotted the woman on her side, immobile. Mel skipped to Alexander with her one boot and, using the chain, lowered him to the floor.

She scanned the garage. "Alexander? Can you hear me? I am going to undo these knots and get you comfortable."

Bloody bubbles came from his mouth and he tried to open one eye. His hair was matted with blood, which ran over his face as she gently eased him onto the floor. His wrists were bleeding and he had burn marks on his chest. He started to shake.

"You're going to be okay, Alexander. I'm here. Don't say anything."

He was trying to use his lips but his body was going into convulsions. She leaned over him to wipe his hair from his face while checking his pulse. She was about to wrap one arm gently around his shoulders, to stop him shaking, but heard a foot dragging behind her.

She moved aside to see the angry man take a swing at her with a large spanner. She stepped into his attack, right under his raised arm and grabbed the spanner to spin him around on his bad knee. He screamed again as she continued to twist his body backwards. She slid on the greasy floor in her sock as he fell out of her grip and disappeared behind a car lift. She heard a loud crash, a mechanical whooshing sound then a dull thud followed by a groan.

A flashing blue light showed through the side door and Inspector Grimble and Sergeant Cadd appeared with batons in hand.

Mel knelt by Alexander, felt his strong pulse and whispered into his ear.

CHAPTER TWENTY-SIX

The sun set behind grass-covered hills drawn with thick charcoal. The empty harbor was a dark-silver mirror.

Moana fed manuka sticks into the fire. She squatted by a bucket of mussels and placed a metal grill with pipis over the embers, their shells about to open. Wiremu and Rawiri relaxed on the blanket and drank from their last brown bottles of beer. They watched the sky turn from crimson to dark purple with only the crackle of the fire to break the silence.

Rawiri sighed as Moana took the pipis off the metal grill and replaced them with mussels. Rawiri watched her adjust her floral dress.

"We were lucky," he said to Wiremu who was playing with the large dark pendant around his neck.

"Our neighbors got it, though." Wiremu shook his head.

"Shouldn't've used such a big truck. Stood out. Not like us."

"Makes you wonder, doesn't it. Will it be us next time?" Wiremu looked over at Moana who stared back at him.

"We only have to be unlucky once. And I really don't want to go back inside again. Ever."

Wiremu nodded. "Same here, brother. Don't know if we should continue with this growing business. We've enough money now to do what we want to do for our iwi. You know, the language classes through the Education Board, my little storefront with the council and getting young Maori kids jobs. Don't want to be remembered as a drug dealer, in prison."

Rawiri and Wiremu held each other's gaze for a long time. They were silent. All they could hear was the fire.

"Love it here." Rawiri gazed at the hills across the water as he breathed in the manuka smoke. "You have to be inside to appreciate the outside."

"What's happened to Ricky, Moana?" Wiremu asked. "You've been real quiet."

Moana kept her eyes on the fire.

"Giving him some space. He's upset. I think he blames us."

"He could've set it himself, destroyed his own crop to stop her blackmail?" Rawiri offered.

"Do you think he'll grow another crop, get back into the business?" Wiremu spoke.

Instead of replying, Moana asked, "Did you hear what happened to our Russian cuzz?"

"Dr. Mel wiped out the Auckland underworld single handed and saved him."

"The curator with the travelling art show?" Rawiri asked.

"Yeah. They kidnapped him."

Rawiri raised his eyebrows. "They kidnapped the curator?"

"Yes. Don't you read the newspaper?"

"And you said he wasn't a cop. Thought he was a bit off."

"But he took my car and delivered the load, didn't he?" Wiremu thought Rawiri was giving Moana an odd look. "What do you think, Moana?"

"He was a nice guy."

"Who? The Flamingo Paradise joker?" Rawiri asked.

"No, the curator. Alexander the Russian. The massage-parlor joker got what he deserved. Bet the cops are mad at Dr. Mel for doing their job."

Wiremu grinned.

"As long as they leave us alone. Do you want me to get more beer?"

"No. Want to open the office tomorrow."

Rawiri pointed his empty beer bottle at his young brother. "No one ever visits you there."

"Sometimes. It only takes one person to change the world."

Rawiri chuckled. "Have you been meditating again?"

Moana laid the plate of cooked shellfish next to the blanket. "You guys, its ready."

CHAPTER TWENTY-SEVEN

"Are you sure you're up to this?" Mel asked as Alexander stopped to catch his breath. He ran his hands through his short-cropped hair and smiled back at her. He wore his denim jacket and blue jeans. His forehead was covered in beads of sweat. In her boots she looked almost as tall as him. She took off her leather jacket.

They were halfway up the trail that started at the end of her street and ran to the top of Mount Eden. Mel was carrying a picnic basket and Alexander a bag with a bottle of champagne, a carton of apple juice and a blanket.

"I've been dreaming of this for three months," he panted, "so we're doing it even if you have to carry me. Besides I've gotten so much rest I need to exercise." He bent over, breathed in deeply, then started the climb again. The grass terraces were dry and easy to walk along as they meandered to the road leading to the summit.

"You want to look at the Manukau and the sunset, or go over to the other crater and look at Rangitoto?"

Mel smiled. "You decide."

"Rangitoto it is. But let's bypass the Castle."

"Are you joking? Sometimes, your sense of humor . . ."

"Oh, I'm looking forwards. Not backwards. I've had a lot of time to think."

Mel followed Alexander along a trail to the smaller crater with a perfect view of the Waitemata Harbor, across to Devonport and, further in the distance, hovering below the purple sky, the symmetrical volcanic cone of Rangitoto. The trees that coated the island appeared deep black.

He came to a particular patch of grass and surveyed the surroundings. There was no one in sight. He put down his bag and, after looking to Mel for approval, laid out the blanket. She dropped her jacket and placed the basket on the edge of the blanket.

Mel put her hands on his arms, then squeezed his shoulders as she looked into his eyes. He could smell the rosemary in her thick dark hair, the scent of her neck, then the taste of her breath and her magic healing fingers.

"You look different. There's something about you." Alexander looked into her amber eyes as their lips touched.

"It's the lighting."

"You've got the glasses, right?" he asked as he unpacked the bottles. "Apple juice? Never seen you drink it."

"And I have the plates and knives and napkins."

They eased onto the blanket next to each other. Mel on her knees, bent over to kiss Alexander again. He could not stop smiling.

"Isn't it going to be too dark soon?" he asked as he helped her unpack the basket.

"Now you ask. If you look over there," she said, pointing to the east, "we'll get a full moon soon."

"Do you know everything?" Alexander asked.

"Get used to it."

"Oh, I already have. Do you want some champagne? Where are the glasses?"

"Just apple juice for now, thanks."

"Oh." Alexander uncorked the champagne and busied himself pouring the drinks while Mel served him a slice of cheese, olives, a piece of a baguette, and a scoop of foie gras on his plate.

"Well, here's to us." Alexander toasted as he raised his glass and clinked Mel's. She sipped her apple juice. "To my savior."

They ate in silence.

They kept looking at each other. It was a comfortable silence.

"How was your visit?" Mel asked. "You haven't spoken about it."

"I didn't think you wanted to hear his name again. After what they put you through."

"True, but tell me anyway."

"Well, I saw Inspector Grimble and his sidekick Sergeant Cadd. What they called tying up loose ends."

"But they'd interviewed you extensively in hospital."

"Yes. Did they ever. But I finally discovered why you weren't prosecuted." He refilled his glass and went to offer her some but she poured herself apple juice. He took a long drink of his champagne.

"As you recall, Superintendent Jarvis, Grimble's boss, was all for charging you—as was the Crown asshole, whatever his name was. Manslaughter and attempted manslaughter. Let me tell you they so badly wanted to prosecute you. Because you used, in their words, excessive force, violence disproportionate to the amount necessary and far beyond that needed in self-defense. But I think they used far longer words than that to justify their charges. And what else? The act was vindictive, dangerous, and heinous in nature. I quote. Then to add insult to injury, they thought I was an unreliable witness as I had a broken occipital bone and one eye closed and suspected brain damage. But I do remember every shock, every hit and who did it."

"Lucky your eye socket wasn't fractured," Mel said. "But I haven't stopped thinking about what I did. The rage, the violence, I scare myself. I'm glad its over. I've a new phase of my life, our lives, to think about."

Alexander took another long drink then made a face with crossed eyes, twisted mouth and his tongue hanging out.

Mel did not laugh. "They kept me up all night. All I wanted to do was see you, but you were being operated on. Then they questioned me again the next day. I was so mad. For all I went through, I should've killed her too, the bitch."

"They told me she's in a home. She had a stroke and they think she'll never recover. Dribbles a lot. No one understands what she says. But that's not the funny part."

"Funny?" Mel spilled her apple juice.

"Will you let me tell the story? When Grimble and Cadd searched her house, in her bedroom they found a silver-framed photo of her and Beverly Jarvis dressed in tennis whites. They looked like best mates. I spied a copy of it on his wall. I mean, *real* mates. Grimble recognized Jarvis's wife and started to look into her finances. He found a bank account where she got the same amount every month, then cross-referenced that with what they had of Barbara Turner's and her brother's accounts, and found a match."

"Grimble told you?"

"Hey, without me almost dying they would never have cracked the case. Although 'cracked' is perhaps not the right word."

"You're so lucky your ribs weren't cracked."

"And I got my Rollei back. Thought it was lost. But they wouldn't show me the photos. From my own camera! But I got the sense they found photos in her brother's house and they were related to what you wanted me to find out at the Flamingo. In fact, there was a strange photo on Grimble's board. I couldn't make it out at the time and didn't want to ask about it. But it was a large cross, X-shaped, with what I thought to be straps, like a medieval torture device. I made a point of looking at it in front of them, but they didn't respond. I got the impression it was found in the garage and the guy you killed used it."

Mel took a sip of her apple juice as she eyed Alexander, a blank expression on her face.

"Now back to the tennis photo. I can only speculate that Grimble took what he found about Jarvis to his former Commissioner buddy. You know, Thompson. Because suddenly Jarvis thought you were a hero, Auckland's number-one crime fighter. In other words, the case against you was dropped. Anyway, Jarvis is retiring, so that's the end of it. Another cover-up, so no scandal."

He refilled his champagne glass and offered Mel some. Again she declined.

"Don't expect a medal or anything."

"Wouldn't want one anyway."

"I think Grimble actually likes me, but I have a feeling he never wants to see me again. Which is fine." He emptied his glass.

"Cost me my self-defense classes. And I got booted out of the Clinic."

"So much for women's lib and stopping violence against women, eh?"

"It's for the best, I think. I like working with my father, and he'll retire soon. It's a lot less stress. And no women coming in with awful injuries."

"I never asked you about Annie. Are you still beating the crap out of her, if you don't have your dojo now?"

"Funny. Did you ever meet Clovis Tibet? Tall, bear-like man with red hair?"

"No."

"You heard about his girlfriend's murder, right? It's something I didn't want to talk about in the hospital."

"Oh, yes. Plum Blossom. I read about it and picked up bits and pieces from all the questioning Grimble gave me. And you took care of her murderer. Why?"

"Well, I first met Clovis over a year ago. It's a long story. But I invited him to a restaurant near my former dojo and on a sort of blind date with Annie."

"I think I can guess what happened."

"Exactly. I didn't dare dream it, but they got on like a house on fire. They completely ignored me, couldn't take their eyes off each other."

"Wasn't he still in mourning?"

"Didn't look like it to me. You know Plum Blossom was a patient of mine. I suppose I can tell you this now. She was very damaged, a psychological mess. She confessed to me she was the one who pushed the remote-control detonator thing that blew up Barbara Turner's husband Terry and the truck. And a lot of innocent people died in that explosion. It haunted her. She was wracked with guilt. She was on a lot of medication and not doing so well. Such a tragedy."

"So what's happened to Annie and Clovis?"

"He's living with her and they are inseparable."

Alexander stared at Mel, went to run his hands through his hair then stopped. He looked at the empty champagne bottle and let out a deep sigh.

"Well, you can't make up stuff like that, can you? I'm glad I'm just a curator, not a crime writer. No one would believe that story." He shook his head. "We need more champagne. Hey, why haven't you had any? We have a lot to celebrate."

"You just noticed? Some detective you are."

"I'm a curator. And soon to be one here in Auckland."

"Alexander, that's great news. When were you going to tell me?"

"It's not official yet, but I got word from the director today after visiting Cook Street. They're going to give me an offer once the Maori show has opened here next month."

Mel raised her apple juice. "That's another reason to celebrate."

"Another reason?" Alexander pressed his eyebrows together.

"Alexander! You haven't worked it out yet?"

"No. What?"

"Remember the time we first made love in your hospital bed?"

"How could I forget? You sat on me. I was helpless."

"Well?"

Alexander turned pale. "Oh."

Lights went off inside his brain. Fireworks. Huge explosions. A nuclear warhead.

"You mean? I thought you were on the pill."

"I thought you'd pull out."

"You were on top of me. What could I do?"

The color returned to his face as he smiled again, broader than ever.

The giant moon rose over Rangitoto.

Mel leaned over to kiss Alexander for a long, long time.